Helen Dickens

A Womans Requital

A Novel: Vol. II.

Helen Dickens

A Womans Requital
A Novel: Vol. II.

ISBN/EAN: 9783337067045

Printed in Europe, USA, Canada, Australia, Japan

Cover: Foto ©Andreas Hilbeck / pixelio.de

More available books at **www.hansebooks**.com

A WOMAN'S REQUITAL.

A Novel.

BY

HELEN DICKENS,

AUTHOR OF "MARRIED AT LAST," "THE MILL WHEEL," "WILD WOOD,"
"THE HOME OF FAITH."

" Though the mills of God grind slowly,
Yet they grind exceeding small
Though with patience He stands waiting,
With exactness grinds He all."

LONGFELLOW.

IN THREE VOLUMES.
VOL. II.

LONDON :
CHARLES J. SKEET, 10, KING WILLIAM STREET
CHARING CROSS.

1881.

A WOMAN'S REQUITAL.

CHAPTER I.

" There's many a flower lies hidden
Deep under ice and snow,
And many a love there burneth,
Whose secret none doth know."

It was Mr. Lovering who spoke. Mr. Lovering's strong hand that was outstretched to me.

I wondered what these women would say if they knew it mended the gates, guided the plough, dabbled in all sorts of work? I jumped up, feeling like an escaped prisoner, a person awakened from a horrible dream.

He was surrounded instantly. Mrs. Fantail and Clem foremost.

"Won't you show *me*?" murmured the fair Clem, casting up her eyes into his face.

"Certainly—at another time. Miss Sharland has been amusing you, it is now my turn to amuse *her*. This way, if you please, Miss Sharland."

He conducted me into the conservatory, and out of that into a fernery, and shut the door.

"What is it?" I inquired.

"Anything you fancy. The ferns, the fountain, the fish. How long had those old vultures been worrying you?" he asked, balancing himself on the edge of the marble basin.

"Not very long; and it does not matter. They know now, so that is over."

"Yes, and you are disgusted and tired. D—— them? Don't look round; are you thinking how you may escape?"

"Something like it. Not from you, but the others—how I could avoid going amongst them again. It looks so cool and quiet under those trees."

He started up and gathered my hands into his.

"Little lonely child, you are braver and nobler than all those women put together; your life is as heaven compared to theirs! How did you get through the dinner?—were you wanting to run off, then?"

"Just for a little, while I could not see you; not after."

"But I thought you wanted to go now? You can see me, can you not?"

" Yes, verily."   Dark though it was, I could see the sparkling eyes and flushed face bent dangerously near to mine.

" Were you planning for me to go, too ?"

" Yes."

" And, by Heaven, I will some day ! —but not to-night—not to-night. If we went off into those woods now, they would raise a hue and cry——"

" Hush ! here is someone."

" Pooh ! they cannot come here. I drew the bolt. It is Clem, or the aunt. Fine women, are they not ?"

" Yes, sir."

" Rather a feeble ' Yes,' Miss Sharland. Not much heart in it. I agree with you: they *are* fine women ! Yet, strangely enough, I prefer talking to you. Who put you up to wearing this ?" touching the feathers round my throat.

" Myself. I had to invent."

" And these?" lifting the cluster of roses on my bosom.

" Peggy."

" Are you generous, Miss Sharland?"

" I hope so, when I have anything to give?"

" Then give me a rose, one that is nearest to you."

I obeyed. I plucked the one that had lain on my neck all the evening.

" It is quite warm," he murmured, kissing it. " See, I place it on my heart, there to remain until——"

Redoubled clattering at the door, and cries of " Mr. Lovering," " William!"

I recognised Miss Miriam's cracked note and Mrs. Fantail's Spanish comb by the light one of the gentlemen held aloft.

They were there in a bevy. The consequence of my situation occurred to me.

"May the devil, etc.!" exclaimed my companion, crushing the rose in his breast; and slipping the bolt, he continued: "My good people, why did you not open the door, instead of making an uproar only excusable if the house were on fire? I had not the least idea *ladies* could be so clamorous!"

Notable discomfiture on the faces, and a titter from the tall guardsman who carried the wax lights.

Miss Miriam's anxiety was so real that she had let slip the youthful expression she was wont to dress her withered countenance in, and I saw the shrivelled, hard skin lifted in nervous puckers round the fallen mouth, which, but for its substantial prop of false teeth, would have curled itself inwards, like any other old woman's.

Her anxious face disturbed me. Was she afraid of her brother?

Perhaps. There was a flash in the deep eye, and the peculiar swing of the coat-tail, that always told me when the squire was roused.

Lynx-eyed Mrs. Fantail was the first to recover her self-possession. That woman's impertinence being of gigantic proportions, it took a great deal to quell it for any time. For *ever* would have been utterly impossible, as it was the head and centre of her existence.

"You have lost one of your roses, Miss Sharland," she proclaimed triumphantly.

The lovely Clem craned her fair neck over her aunt's shoulder and smiled—such a smile as innocence never gave birth to.

Mr. Lovering saw it, saw that every eye was levelled at me.

"Remarkably sharp sight you have, Miss Kirkham; excellence only equalled by beauty. Miss Sharland gave one of her roses to—the fishes."

A scornful laugh from Clem.

"Do hold the light nearer, Mr. Vaughan," she pleaded, bending over the basin.

I defined her meaning as I heard a slight hiss from between Mr. Lovering's teeth.

"My sight is not so good as you supposed, for I cannot see a single trace of a rose, Mr. Lovering."

He laughed, a short, sharp sound, with nothing of hilarity in it.

"Very likely not, Miss Kirkham. Fishes are no wiser than some ladies, and when they can, resort to artificial means to increase their beauty. Most probably these fish, silly things ! thought the colour of the rose leaves might brighten their gills, so they have *eaten* them. I know *you* can understand their feelings and sympathise with them in the pardonable deception !"

He placed his hand on her arm. With a sharp scream of rage, not pain, she drew back.

" You hurt me, Mr. Lovering !"

" A thousand pardons, my dear Miss Clem ; I had no idea you were so tender !"

Lanky Mr. Vaughan was here seized with such violent inward twitchings that he jerked the candle out of its socket, and shot it in amongst the gold fishes, leaving us in darkness.

This exploit elicited a genuine laugh from the master.

"Do you know whether candles are good for fish, Vaughan ?"

" I do not.   Ask Miss Kirkham."

But Miss Clem had gone.

"Move on, ladies, move on !" called Mr. Lovering ; and there was a general stir.   " Well, witch," he said, turning to me, where I sat under the shadow of an aged fern.   " Don't look at me reproachfully ; I did my best.   I ought never to have brought you here, but I could not resist.   I knew something was wrong, by a tightness under the left side of my waistcoat all the time I sat with those men, and then, when I found you encompassed by that herd, I could not let you suffer another moment."

I saw the light of passion gathering in

his face again. Now was my time to go.

I rose and moved towards the door, he little knew how reluctantly.

" You are going ?"

" Yes, Mr. Lovering ; it is better for you that I should go."

" So it is ; right, child, right. What a wise little head ; what a cool little hand ! Grace, I would trust you in a great difficulty. You will help me when I am in sorrow ?"

" Yes, sir."

" What a collected ' Yes, sir !' Just as if——there, run along, run along !"

I did.

No one noticed my entrance, and I took a seat near a table whereon lay a number of splendid views of Rome. In these I soon became interested. Most of the company were gathered round the piano, at which Miss Clem sat singing "Non e' vere," and throwing passionate glances at Mr. Vaughan.

Mr. Lovering had entered some moments after I did. He had gone round and come through the house.

We were divided by the whole length of the room, and he made no attempt to join me, though I felt he had looked round and found my hiding-place.

Not long was I allowed to enjoy it in peace. Miss Miriam and Mr. Hastings came up.

" I am glad you have found these views, my dear," kindly remarked Miss Miriam, evidently now troubled with no fears, " for I am sure you will appreciate them. My brother brought them home after one of his wanderings. He used to be very fond of travelling at one period, and I think his greatest trouble was when he could not go out with Dr. Livingstone."

Mr. Hastings remarked, " Indeed !" and gaped stupidly at me.

Miss Miriam hurried away to talk to Mrs. Duckworth, and Miss Clem continued to scream and ogle the men.

She stopped ; and I heard Mr. Lovering's voice above all others bestowing rapturous praise on the vocalist.

Little Mr. Hastings now asked me to sing.

" You cannot say you do not, Miss Sharland ?"

" No."

" Then you will ? You have a singing face."

" I did not know you were a fortune-teller, Hastings, and I must be permitted to differ from you. Miss Sharland's face is at present anything but a singing one. Perhaps you don't sing ?"

"She does, William," said Miss Miriam, hurrying up, "and will sing for us now, I am sure. It will afford us all such pleasure."

What could I do but agree ?

Mr. Lovering was conversing with Mr. Hastings, and Miss Miriam escorted me to the piano.

These ladies never compelled their brother to perform any office they were equal to. They were so much older, that it seemed natural to them to take the lead, and for another, and perhaps better reason —they could not always depend upon his humour.

When I took my seat at the instrument I heard a murmur from Mrs. Fantail, who probably expected some catchie song of renown three years before, or a feeble imitation of a well-worn operatic air, with variations that sent cold shivers through you.

I made my choice. A simple, tuneful song, of rare pathos and exquisite harmony, telling a story quick and thrilling— " der Scheffer."

I had never sung in such a large room before, or to so many people.

I cannot plead nervousness ; I felt nothing but keen pleasure at the tone of the splendid piano, and perfect confidence in my own powers.

My voice rose steady, rich, and filled the room from corner to corner ; there was no flaw, no thinness. I heard it with satisfaction ; I would make him listen.

Not always does the most powerful

voice evoke the greatest attention, or leave
the most genuine pleasure in the memory.

With skilful management a voice of
moderate compass may achieve great success with a very critical audience. This my
father had impressed upon me, and taught
me how to modulate and expand with the
truest effect, keeping always in view the
story being told.

Thus I had sung from my childhood,
putting my own heart in the place of
others, feeling and depicting their joys
and sorrows as if they were my own.

My father had praised my rendering of
some descriptive music, and said I inherited
my mother's talent.

My mother had one tiny regret—that
she had not made the stage her profession.
Something of this latent theatrical genius
I had imbibed, therefore I was not

astonished at the conclusion of my song to hear, uttered in spiteful accents :

" Quite startling—positively theatrical !"

I returned to my former seat, and combined occupation of looking at the pictures and talking to Mr. Hastings.

I recognised the square shoulders of the master, who with averted face was talking to old Mrs. Morland.

Had he liked my song ? If he would only turn his face I could decide for myself.

These and other thoughts crowded my brain, and made Mr. Hastings's incessant chatter very tedious to endure.

I had a vague notion he was doing what is termed flirting, and I regretted that his stupendous efforts in this line should have been so thrown away.

I now noticed that the company were separating, and footmen came in with whispered announcements, seeking for some special object in the assembly.

I would go.

I caught sight of Miss Miriam, and to her I went.

She glanced up rather playfully.

" Well, my dear ?"

" I should like to go, Miss Miriam."

" Certainly, my dear. Say good-night to anyone you please, and then I will go upstairs with you."

Surely she was making a fuss over me. There was only one person in the room whom I cared to bid good-bye to, and that I had better not do.

" No, Miss Miriam ; I can slip through that door and find my own way upstairs. Good-night !"

" Ah ! I understand — rather flurried. I can remember my own feelings when your age, and we are very impetuous. You must not mind, though such sudden conquests are enough to make any young thing nervous."

I stared in amazement.

" Conquests, Miss Miriam ?"

" Certainly. Was there ever a clearer one, silly child ?"

" Why so ?" inquired Mr. Lovering, who had come up.

" Here, William, you are generally considered a good judge of people's intentions by their manners and actions, what do you make of Mr. Hastings ? Is it not a clear case of love at first sight ?"

My face became hot, water rushed into my eyes, and I could not raise them.

Was there ever confusion more intense, more provoking?

Miss Miriam's question received no answer.

"You must consider Mr. Lovering's silence as an assent, my dear; and now good-night. There is Wilcox."

She kissed me, and patted me encouragingly on the arm.

I made no return; I saw the open door, and I hailed it joyfully as a means of escape. But I bungled, my fingers were weak, and the door heavy.

A firm hand clasped over mine, and the door yielded.

In the hall I managed to say :

"Good-night, Mr. Lovering."

"To be sure; *good*-night, Miss Sharland. The carriage will be round in five minutes."

He was gone directly.

When I came down the carriage was there, and in state I was ushered into it, and driven home.

No sign was there of the master.

CHAPTER II.

" ' My heart, I fain would ask thee,
    What call'st thou love, expound ?'
' Two souls with one thought between them,
    Two hearts with one pulse-bound.' "

THE drive home in the moonlight was pleasant. Alone in the great carriage, the soft cushions, the easy motion, all served to lull me like a tired child. I recollected the events of the evening with terror. What was the meaning of it? how would, how *could* it end? I knew what I hoped, how my silly heart beat. I strove for calmness, I prayed for the revival of that strong common sense that had hitherto been mine.

What had I done?

Allowed an elderly, ugly man to deprive me of my very will, to render himself the one being with whom I saw the prospect of a happy future for myself, a life worth living for. I felt that my strong, wild nature was subdued, that I had lost what was my defence, my stronghold, my independence. Never again could I act or think for myself alone.

Could I be mistaken in his meaning; was I crediting him with motives he did not entertain? I was very ignorant in the ways of the world: a child in many respects.

Was his kindness and thought for me no more than what he would feel for any other woman similarly placed?

Perhaps. But what meant the self-conscious whisper that I was something more to him? why did Memory reproduce so exactly every word and look, losing none of the tenderness displayed at the time? A woman who is not wicked may always trust her own heart in such matters. Mine was aching when the carriage stopped at the gate.

Peggy was waiting very near the door, it seemed to me, by the instantaneous manner of its opening.

"I have set your supper, Miss Grace; you are one as needs a little something before they go to bed."

"I am not inclined for any, Peggy."

"Have you enjoyed yourself, Miss Grace?"

"Yes, thank you."

I thought perhaps my manner was too

abrupt, so I sat down and told the worthy old soul something of the doings at the Manor.

I was amply rewarded for my effort by her pleasure.

I was early up the next morning, and went singing on my way. My doubt of the preceding night had tortured me, but knowing full well what would be expected of me by those who hired me, I banished it, rebraced my mind, and strove to find in sunny nature the joy no mortal could deprive me of.

Every teacher has trials and disappointments, and some black sheep amongst her flock. My pupils were no better than any other persons, perhaps not so bright. Some had come to me with sorry recommendations from loving relations and friends. Possessing some slight knowledge of character, I taught each differently, according to his or her capacity. I had what is termed tact, and the issue was that they learnt and did me credit. I knew it was to my advantage to turn out good players, and I spared no efforts to render them such. Those learning the violin were simply wasting their time. They would never succeed in drawing any melody out of the instrument, and I dreaded the lessons.

The holidays were at hand once more, and I counted my gains.

Reader, I was not by any' means insolvent, and all I besought God for was—health.

The day after the party, Mr. Lovering had gone from home, into Wales, they said, and I had not seen him.

Nothing could have been more cooling

—more damping—to one's affection ; and I felt a return of the old indiffer- ence.

I had only one more lesson to give, and this on the violin. Imagine my relief when I was informed that, in consequence of her aunt's death, Miss Moss would not take her lesson.

I almost rushed down the steps, for- getting that some one was certain to be watching from behind a blind. When I reached the corner of the square, I saw Mr. Leete go whirling past in his gig. He did not see me; his face was white and earnest.

An idea occurred to me; I would go and see the Leetes. I knew their house, one of the oldest in Danver. Its face fronted the market-place, and its garden ran down to the river and joined the mill,

standing white and gaunt, the only mill
in Danver.

It was one of the cleanest-looking houses
in the town. The steps were white, and
worn with the tread of feet. A couple
of bells and an enormous brass plate
garnished the door, bearing the name of
" Leete," which constant scouring was rendering fainter.

An elderly domestic opened the door,
and showed me into a pleasant sitting-room
covered in clean holland.

Not three minutes did Mrs. Leete keep
me waiting. She looked even prettier
without her bonnet. Her delicate beauty
was enhanced by the cap of black lace and
rich violet velvet she wore.

Her kiss was given readily and tenderly,
and I appreciated it. She was the very
first *mother* who had ever kissed me.

"Come and take your things off, my dear ; Mr. Leete would be quite angry if I let you go."

"But I must leave in time to reach home before dark."

"You shall ; there is plenty of time for that. My daughters are out at present ; one shopping, the other at school. We take tea at six, dinner at one."

So chatted Mrs. Leete, as she took me upstairs.

The comfort and neatness of that town-house, with a large family in it and only two servants, spoke volumes for the energy and management of its mistress.

By degrees the family came in.

First Miss Leete, very pretty, delicate and sensitive, like her mother. Then Mary, stronger, plainer, cleverer ; and, in ones and twos, the five sons, all well

grown, good-looking, and moderately intelligent.

The one that seemed to me the most
reliable—the most like the father—was
Mary; and oddly enough, I saw she was
not very popular with the others, nor did
she care particularly for them.

The big brothers petted her in a silly,
good-natured fashion; and Miss Leete
snubbed her whenever she got an opportunity.

This family interested me.

The dining-room was large, and furnished
very plainly. Its two long rows of heavy
chairs gave it a strange look to my unaccustomed eye. But when they were, some
of them, pulled out and set round the long
table, occupied by the sons and daughters,
it made all the difference.

The conversation was pleasant, but

shallow ; they were not clever, the Leetes, none took after the father, save the youngest ; and several times I saw her short upper-lip lifted scornfully at some affected or silly speech, in ꞁa manner that betokened no good for the future. This bird would never stay long in the same nest with the others. She sat next to her father, and though extremely reserved and cold in her manner, I saw that her watch-fulness was unceasing. She loved this parent as such natures alone are able to love, with an intensity that is anguish to themselves.

I thought how, in a few years—very few —for she was almost a woman now, though they did not know it—she would love some man ; not in the feeble, caressing style common to women, but in the grand, noble fashion her mind approved, with a devotion that would stand any test, last her whole life.

I sat next to Mr. Leete, and he paid me such kind attention that I felt slightly embarrassed. He called me " my dear," as if I had belonged to him, and unconsciously tendered to me that very protection that wins a haughty, proud woman's earnest regard.

The sons had all the good appearance, without the father's strength, either mentally or physically.

After tea I played and sang for them, and presently proposed going home.

" The boys shall go with you, my dear ; and one of the girls, if you like."

I knew he made the latter suggestion out of a sense of delicacy, thinking I might not like the male escort alone. Somehow I did not fancy pretty Annie Leete half so well as her sister, and hoped she might express a desire to go. I soon found out that Mary was considered the family pack-horse; to carry any load Annie disliked.

" Mary, get dressed ; it won't hurt you," said Mrs. Leete, in a burst of authority and disparagement.

Miss Leete had settled herself to her fancy-work.

Mary rose, a quiet smile of scornful obedience curling her small mouth. Mary Leete was by no means well-looking; but she would grow up a fine-figured, sensible woman. Her self-control enabled her to hide her feelings, and her principle was so excellent, that she performed whatever was required of her without a murmur or pout.

Mrs. Leete had the notion that children should be kept down.

Mary was rapidly raising her proud head out of her mother's reach, and the good lady's ineffectual efforts to regain her leading-strings were very amusing.

Mary neared the door and spoke. The tone of voice was good, sweet, and full —enough to denote the passion that lay beneath. The words had the easy utterance that promises a continuance and a command of language.

" Why the walk is supposed to be better for me than for Annie I cannot see. I have already walked to Sunney Hill four times, and only a week to-morrow the accident happened to my foot. My lessons are still three parts to do. But I will go, for I like your mandate *this* time, mother ; and I know I shall prove a pleasanter companion to Miss Sharland."

There was a titter from the two remaining sons—Arthur and Patrick.

Mr. Leete said, " What's this, mamma ?"

" Only Mary grumbling," replied Mrs. Leete, looking terribly taken aback.

I saw a perplexed expression on Mr. Leete's face.

" Mary, you should not grumble to your mother."

" I am not grumbling, papa dear."

" Well, well; perhaps you will explain why you are likely to prove a pleasanter companion than your sister ?"

" I can do that easily, papa. In the first place, I like and know more about the things Miss Sharland takes an interest in ; therefore we are not likely to waste half the time hunting for a mutual topic. Secondly, I can get over a stile, and am not afraid of a cow, or my constitution.

Thirdly, I can see when I have said enough."

Thereupon she closed the door, leaving us all in terrible straits.

CHAPTER III.

"Impose not a burden on others which thou canst
not bear thyself."

MESSRS. PATRICK and ARTHUR were choking
with laughter. Miss Leete was shedding
tears upon her satin-work. Mrs. Leete
was boiling with rage. Mr. Leete and I
were convulsed with mirth, which we both
suppressed from a sense of consideration
toward the mother and daughter.

I might have made some remark expressive of regret at taking Miss Mary out,
and protested my willingness to go alone.
But I saw that it only wanted just a very

little more to raise a tumult, in which everyone would fare worse than Mary. She would retire quietly to her bedroom, and there amuse herself with her store of information, while the others chewed the cud of mortification in the sitting-room.

I also wanted to improve my acquaintance with this strange young lady, in whom I surmised the entire brains of the family were centred.

Miss Leete having wiped her eyes and been hugged to her father's ample breast, attended me to the bedroom, where she sat sucking her lips.

She was extremely pretty, and dreadfully conscious of it. Her delicacy was a fortune to her, and her parents were silly enough to pamper her and be imposed upon time after time.

Before I was dressed Mary entered.

Her attire was very simple; indeed, shabby.

" Papa is vexed with you, Mary."

" Of course. He would cut off one of my ears if the law would permit him, and if he fancied it would shorten the pangs of your vexation. What sort of soothing syrup is it to be this time, Annie?—a pug, or a new riding-whip? Flowers have a beauty in the window—a horse's head in gold. Just cry yourself sick, faint twice, have one stye on your eye, and you'll get whichever you like, or both."

Shaking with rage, Miss Leete drew herself up for another sting.

" It is to be hoped you won't meet anybody, Mary; you are really not fit to be seen!"

" On the contrary, I hope I may meet every person I know, especially that ad-

mirer of yours with the spindle legs. You
should ask him whether he would like to
come and hang up in the garden to scare
Mr. Bland's pigeons. With regard to my
appearance, I think Miss Sharland will
agree with me that it is wonderful, considering that every single article on my
back has been worn more than half out by
either you or your mother. I was only
wondering, as I went to school this morning, whose bowels of compassion would be
moved in my behalf next. Mother's, I
suspect; there is that cloth dress with the
yellow spots and blackberry buttons, which
I am destined to get inside of. You,
owing to your remarkable ability in the
dressmaking line, will be called upon for
your valuable opinion, and, mindful of my
broad shoulders, and our last sisterly tiff,
will suggest enormous puffings at the top

of the sleeves, and a corresponding one
round the bottom of the skirt. By the
time you have done experimenting upon
me, you will be qualified for the post of
' costumier extraordinary ' to her majesty.
If the Danver population only knew, they
would reverence me as I deserve, for I am
a living, visible proof of how old things
may be made new, and how the seeds of
dissension are painstakingly sown in a
family possessing at least six Bibles, each
and all recommending that—we love one
another."

My dressing had not progressed during
this speech, I was so engrossed listening.
This girl tickled one's ears strangely and
charmingly.

Miss Leete had not understood half
Mary had said, but from habit she would

go down and complain of her unkindness
and rudeness.

Most sedately Mary preceded us to the
sitting-room, the commanding walk and
well-carried head stamping her at once as
a lady, and one who might, by reason of
her cleverness and sharp tongue, grow up
disagreeable if worried.

Already she had perfected herself in the
art of wordy warfare, and maintained her
calmness and temper very provokingly.
Her face, when seen under the big mush-
room hat, was full of lurking humour and
inward satisfaction.

Mrs. Leete avoided speaking to her,
and even her father did so restrainedly,
because he knew he was expected to re-
prove, and he did not desire to do so.
How much wiser it would have been to
have put matters on the proper footing,

and owned that priority of birth did not always guarantee an advancement in intellect.

Very kindly indeed did the Leetes part with me, and assured me at any time they would be happy to see me. Then, escorted by Arthur and Mary, I turned homewards.

Patrick, who was handsome, like his mother, silly and conceited, had gone to drill. This Mary told me.

Arthur was the youngest, and very amorous. Altogether Mary's matter-of-fact remarks did not come amiss from time to time. Her " Now, Arthur, don't be a goose!" had the most salutary effect. The conversation was made up of odds and ends of Danver chatter till we reached the meadows by the river, and here we met two ladies.

Mary chuckled.

" Arthur, how does your heart feel ?
—here are the Pountenys !"

Arthur's dark face was a dusky red.

" Mary, you hold your tongue !"

" Certainly.   Fleet as it is, it is a very
sluggard compared with Mamma Pounteny's.   Arthur, listen, and never mind
your moustache !   All the hairs are lying
the right way, and that striped shirt makes
you lovely.   I will go on with Miss
Sharland, and you can come after
me ?"

" Yes ; capital idea, Mary, if Miss Sharland don't mind."

I nearly laughed.

" Not in the least ; pray join your
friends."

I wondered what effect he supposed his
feeble charms were likely to have upon

me, to whom a certain ugly face was the only one in which I had ever seen a glimmer of light.

I glanced at the girl by my side. She had passed the Pountenys with a stiff move, and left Arthur with them. There was a scornful expression on her face now.

" You don't like those people, Miss Mary ?"

" No, I don't. Annie does, because they dress well and talk tall. But they will give that brother of mine the lesson he needs before they finish with him ; so perhaps I should not dislike the means to an end."

" I do not understand you."

" I did not expect you would ; but you will easily enough when I have explained. Arthur is in love with Miss Pounteny, and he has not wit enough to perceive that they only tolerate him."

"Time may induce them to alter their opinion."

"No, it cannot, because the fault rests with his birth. We are not the aristocracy of Danver, Miss Sharland, and, consequently, looked down upon. That does not signify; but I would that my brother had the sense to keep clear of the people above us, and so escape insult and ridicule."

"They may not look at it in the light you do."

"They do not, or they would never place themselves in the position to be snubbed. Then, when they receive what they have gone out of their way to obtain, they are furious; but even that wears off, and they plunge in head-first again."

" What would you do under similar circumstances ?"

" Profit by experience, and commit no two errors of a like nature."

" Will you tell me how old you are, Miss Mary ?"

She smiled, and instantly became more like her father. Their smile was the brightest I ever saw ; rushing over the stern faces like a sunbeam, and rendering them almost too bright to look at. Her teeth were even, strong, and beautiful in colour, showing a good constitution.

" Fifteen. I wish I had been born after Robert."

" Don't; you will be more useful coming at the last."

The conversation then turned to literature, and I was amazed at her varied information and clear judgment.

I did not imagine one of those brothers knew a quarter as much. No marvel she sneered at them, and resented the pressure they subjected her to.

I could see Upholland standing out from the trees : ten minutes more and I should be home.

"Will you turn back, or will you come home with me, Miss Mary ?"

" I'll go back, though I should dearly like to go home with you. Some other time perhaps, Miss Sharland, I may come."

" Certainly. I hope to see you often ; I am sure we shall be friends. Are you afraid to go back alone ?"

" No. Very likely I may meet Arthur, that is, if that girl has not completely turned his head—which is addled sufficiently already."

We parted. When I reached the top of

the hill I looked back, and such good use had she made of the time, that she was half-way through the meadows.

Peggy met me at the gate. A gentleman had called, and left no name.

"Then he cannot have had any special message, so it does not matter."

"What do you think they say, Miss Grace?—that the master is going abroad."

The blood curdled round my heart, and the pretty old house, the leafy wood, the fresh fields, all seemed to lose their beauty.

" It may not be true," continued the old woman, while making the parsley into a neat bunch; "but that is what they say on the farm."

I breathed more freely, and leaving her plucking, I wandered away into the orchard.

At the cherry-tree I stopped.

Could it have spoken, its opinion would have proved valuable. Under its branches had been enacted a scene that might have turned the aspect of affairs if reviewed by uninterested people. It is a cowardly mistake to look at things from only one point—naturally you choose the pleasantest to yourself—and I sifted my brains with care to try and find another motive for his conduct than the one my heart affirmed. I loved him, and I did not blush or cringe at the discovery. It is a woman's lot to love and be loved once, if no more. If this was my time, if the hour of my agony had come, I must endure it with fortitude, and not permit the first love of my life to deprive me of the delicacy which ought to be every woman's birthright.

Whether I loved in vain or not, I must

hide my feelings, and manage that others did not learn my secret.

That battle took me an hour to fight; at the end of it I saw him walking by the edge of the wood.

Then I went in and to bed. I prayed and I slept.

CHAPTER IV.

"You call them thieves and pillagers; but know
  They are the winged wardens of your farm,
Who from the cornfields drive the insidious foe."

My holidays were at hand, and I derived no scanty satisfaction from that fact. I wanted the rest: my appetite failed, my eyes became brighter, and Peggy fidgeted after me incessantly.

She, kind creature, innocently imagined that it was the heat and constant tramping that had knocked me up. I knew that my mind was vastly more afflicted than my body. The treatment I subjected myself to was severe.

I mercilessly laid bare every fault I possessed—my youth, my poverty; and told myself that I had been a fool, and deluded myself with a persistent stupidity for which there could be no pardon. I had unbidden taken to my heart a hope, and with it sweetened my life. I had woven deftly and cunningly a fabric, and when exposed to the light every thread in it was—Love. It was only when I began to unravel it that I knew the loom had been my own heart.

He had never been near me; if he cared, he would come. I caught the infection and avoided him, though the corn-fields attracted me powerfully, and I longed to creep up the hedgeways and gather the

poppies and corn-bottles that grew between.

Inside, the larks and corncrakes made
merry, the small birds swayed and twittered
on the yellow stems, the crickets chirped
through the cracks in the baked earth.
And I denied myself, for I thought I
might meet him, and one look would undo
all my work. The cure was not yet complete. So I idled in the garden, and let
my violin tell, in its own pathetic tones,
my sorrow.

It was hot again, hotter than during
hay-time, and man and beast seemed to
sink under it partially. I felt weak and
inert. Peggy proposed a trip to the seaside. The plan did not meet with my
approbation. I was suffering just about
enough. To banish myself was too much
agony at once.

One morning, when I awoke, added to the buzz of bees and insects was another sound—a burring, whirring noise, with a click to it.

"What is that sound, Peggy?" I asked, when she brought me a glass of milk at six o'clock.

"Them grand new reaping - machines the master got, and paid a lot of money for. They are cutting the corn. Have you slept at all, Miss Grace?"

"All night, Peggy."

I could not tell her that I had been awake at least a dozen times, and dreamt when I slept.

"Will you drink this now, Miss Grace?"

"In a moment, Peggy. Just set it down."

She did so, and left me. Then I turned my face into the pillow and sobbed.

I was sick and silly, and I mourned for the golden grain that had so bountifully sheltered the songsters, and amongst which the wind had made such pleasant music, as only a tired, yearning heart can. I felt ashamed of the salt tears as soon as they were shed. But they did me good.

To-day, for the first time for many, I considered my appearance—took some trouble to dress becomingly. My face was thin and pale, and round my temples I could trace blue veins.

The sound of the reaping-machines never ceased, nor did my longing to behold them.

I sought employment from Peggy, and found it—slicing beans for dinner. I took the dish and sat out on the slab, within sight of the harvesters and sound of the poultry, who, with the snowy pigeons, soon gathered round me. Peggy tied a large apron over my clean dress. The dish was nearly full, and the speckled hen had got into one of the milk-cans, when Peggy arrived.

"Miss Grace, here is that gentleman again asking to see you."

"What is his name?"

"I never asked him. He would not tell it last time, so I did not think it worth while to ask this."

I got up and went into the house. At the very door of the sitting-room Peggy caught me by the skirt and pulled me back.

"You've got the apron on, Miss Grace."

So I had, bib and all.

Laughing at Peggy's face of dismay, I entered the room, but the smile fled directly I beheld Mr. Hastings. I guessed what

had brought him : he was going to pro-
pose.

We know women who positively like
being proposed to, and for that purpose
deliberately lure men on when they do not
care a straw for them. We are not of
that order. There is not a more delicate
or painful duty than being obliged to tell
a good, honourable man you cannot be his
wife.

I felt the awkwardness of my position,
and fervently hoped the ordeal might soon
be over. Poor Mr. Hastings ! he tried to
talk upon indifferent subjects, and explained
where he was staying, with a doctor at
Grately.

It came ere long, that question which to
every man and woman is the great crisis
in life. Nearly every man asks it differently—some are too cowardly even to

ask it at all: prefer to let the woman's heart ache itself into numbness, and then conclude that she could not have ever really cared.

Thank God such men are few, or the cowardly blow falls upon women who can suffer quietly and live broken-hearted! Be that as it may, we do not often hear of such men receiving the punishment merited.

Mr. Hastings was a timid man, and naturally he cringed when offering to devote himself for ever to another human being, particularly one with tolerably persuasive powers and a strong will.

This was my first offer, and I knew no set phrase. I uttered my feelings, simply and shortly.

" I am sorry you care for me, Mr. Hastings, for I cannot marry you."

" You do not love me, then ?"

" No."

" Perhaps you might get to love me in time ?"

"No, I should not," I answered shivering. "I know my own heart. I could *never* care for you as I ought to do. Do not tempt me, for it *is* a temptation to one poor and friendless. You deserve a better wife than I should make you."

Mentally I contrasted him with Mr. Lovering, and I felt that good, worthy, commendable though he might be, he could never be my master.

Looking at it from a worldly point, my lack of affection for this man was to be regretted. He was rich, and sufficiently amiable to be a pleasant companion. Married to him, my cares—of one kind at least—would have ended.

And he loved me! I was woman enough

to discover that—indeed, he made no effort to conceal it.

Some men govern themselves too well to allow their weakness to overtake them, and become, if anything, colder in the presence of their love. This may be remarkably clever, and denote a strong mind, but it is excessively puzzling and quite unnecessary.

In loving some woman well enough to cherish and protect her all your life, we can see nothing to be ashamed of, or mysterious about, and it causes some dreadful errors that can never be corrected. A girl subjected to this silence and coldness will doubt her own heart, and believing herself mistaken, set up affected indifference.

Mr. Hastings being but a sorry actor, his passion was suffered to flow on unchecked. Good little man ! he loved, and he was not ashamed of it ; and he had (as is often the case), no tribe of pauper relations hanging like millstones round his neck, whom to keep in idleness and plenty, he was obliged to break some other girl's heart.

His weak pleading touched me, and the temptation to secure for myself ease and affluence was strong. I will not deny it. Yet my battle with the world had not robbed me of my sense of justice, or deadened my conscience. I *dare not* sell myself—and I loved. When a woman of determination once does that, every other argument goes for naught.

" Please go away, Mr. Hastings ; you have my final answer."

He went, very sickly-looking, very de- jected, and so ended my first offer. When he had gone I cried.

I felt as though I had done a very wicked, heartless thing to refuse him. I did not know then that hearts were easily mended.

CHAPTER V.

"The sunny days are coming on,
And ere they are departed,
We will enjoy them, aye, we will,
My friend, my trusty-hearted."

THE harvest progresses, and I see the waving corn cut down and the birds turned away for a time homeless.

I regret all this necessary devastation. I shall miss the lights and shades that played on the fields, the music the wind made in the oats at nightfall. To a solitary person Nature has a language more expressive than any tongue, and with her unceasing generosity she is kind to those who seek her companionship.

Mr. Lovering was at home, for I had seen his straw hat towering above the others, and heard his strong voice shouting orders to some far-off workers. We avoided each other.

Sunday morning.

The sun arose hot and bright, shining directly upon my bed. I lay awake, enjoying the perfect quiet that reigned, till the church bell called to early prayers.

This set me thinking of church. I had not been for months; my simple attire had not reminded the charitable people of Holland of my existence. Should I go to-day and thank God that I still lived? I could do that at home, and the surest way to express my gratitude for a continuance of health and strength was to use them properly. That I firmly believed I did.

If I went, I did not know where to sit. The Upholland pew was, perhaps, amongst those set apart for the Manor servants. Could I endure the gaze of those grey eyes for three hours? No! But—I hid my face in the pillow—if I could get into some part of the church unseen I might look at him, and that would be no harm.

When the time came I dressed. What a simple toilet! any of the farmers' daughters or servants were superb by comparison. A soft creamy dress and jacket ; a black chip bonnet with jet clasps and gauze strings, and long black gloves.

The dress I had made myself, likewise trimmed the bonnet after one for a young widow.

" Going to church, Miss Grace ?"

"Yes, Peggy; I think so."

"I wish you had some colour in your cheeks."

It was useless listening to Peggy's laments; they had been pretty general of late. My paleness was a constant eyesore to her.

It was nearer through the fields, and cut off a good portion of the dusty road. I went that way. They had cut avenues amongst the corn, and to my amazement I discovered that in the last field the cutting had not been taken through. There was a large piece of standing grain between me and the stile.

Push my way through I would not. There was only one course : turn back and make for the road higher up. I was tired, hot, and vexed. The bells sounded fainter, as if they intended dropping off altogether

21—2

soon, and since the sun had been scorching my back my desire to worship had marvellously diminished.

I began to think I had been very silly to come out. I repented of my decision; I would return, but prior to doing so I would sit down and recover my breath. I selected one of the sheaves, and pulling it out of the sun's direct rays, seated myself thereon.

I had a fan in my pocket, and with my sunshade up, my gloves off, and my back comfortably supported, I certainly might have been worse off. A rabbit came out and looked at me curiously, jerking its tail, and twitching its whiskers in the sunlight. Suddenly it rushed away in hot haste, and I wondered what could have disturbed it; there was no sound.

In a couple of minutes I heard one—a

regular patter, and Rap came up wag-
ging his bushy tail. His master could not
be far off. My heart beat; I was caught
in a trap; I must face him.

Better do it partially hidden, where I
could make play with my parasol. My
legs felt as jerky as bunnie's tail. Rap
came fawning upon me, putting his curled
head into my lap, and blinking his bright
eyes. My caress was quiet, but I kissed him,
one long, loving kiss! I thought the brute
knew how it was with me, for he stretched
himself by my side. All tremor ceased,
and I became calm. Happily I possess
that power; when desperate I can check
all outward show of emotion.

His voice was constrained, his utterance
short and rather snubby.

"How do you do, Miss Sharland? I
had no idea I should find you here."

I laughed.

" I am quite aware of that."

" Had you surmised it you would have instantly taken another direction ?"

" To tell the truth, I am here against my will, so there is little chance of us proving pleasant companions."

He was chewing a straw with energy.

" I don't know that ; why should we not pass a few minutes in sociable converse ?   I am little loath to discard the opportunity ; fate is not always so generous to me.   It would have been more my luck to have encountered Miss Rutland or—one of my sisters.   How have you been lately ?"

I let my sunshade slip over my shoulder, and look up.

" All right," I reply.

" All right ! all wrong, you mean !

What has made you so pale and thin ?"

" The heat, I suppose," I make haste to answer, trying to avoid the searching eye.

I hear him give a weary sigh, as he arranges a bundle of corn by my side and sits down.

" Now, Miss Sharland, in the absence of a more worthy confessor, you had better confess to me."

" I don't think the character of confessor becomes you, sir."

" Why not ?"

" You belong too much to the world to gain the confidence of the wretched."

He laughed.

" You would say I reek of the good things of this life, and savour not at all of sacking and ashes. I am not of opinion that tormenting the body purifies the soul. I can tell of a keener torture—self-denial."

"Are you practising it?"

"Yes; but—I am not sure that I shall continue to do so. Do you think that the innocent should suffer for the guilty, even to perfect a great work, Miss Shar-land?"

"Certainly not; at any rate, the choice should be given them. We have no right to punish each other unlawfully."

"I agree with you. I don't think I will make a martyr of myself any more, nor of anyone else."

He had taken my hands in his, and amused himself bending my fingers.

The sour look had gone out of his face, his eyes had a soft, steady light in them.

"I have not seen you for a long time," he remarked, presently.

"No. I avoided you, because I do not like being snubbed, and you are snubbish now and again."

"Nonsense! you don't understand. What makes your face so white? Those black strings surely."

So saying, he untied them.

"They have nothing to do with it. I am rather done up with the heat, and so have not been able to eat very much."

"What do you drink—wine?"

My eyes opened wide in astonishment. Where did he suppose wine was to come from?

"No; I hardly ever take any. I like water better, only just now there is no getting it cold."

"Put ice in it."

Here was another difficulty.

" I have not got any."

" Umph ! From this time forth consider yourself the possessor of plenty. I will send it to you."

" Thank you, but——"

" No 'buts,' if you please. Can you not accept such a trifle from me ? Am I so obnoxious to you that the acceptance of the least favour is disagreeable ? Or are you too proud ?"

" Too proud ! How ridiculous such pride must seem to you, who know my poverty."

" It does not ; I admire you for it. But admiration to you is no novelty. Perhaps the consideration necessary for weighing the pros and cons of a proposal causes your paleness."

" What do you mean, Mr. Lovering ?"

"Exactly what I have said. A proposal."

Instantly the image of little Mr. Hastings rose in my mind, and I blushed the colour of a peony. He was watching me, and I hated myself for colouring. It was only momentary: soon I was whiter than before.

"I appear to have made a painful remark, Miss Sharland. Is it not a case for congratulation?"

"If you allude to Mr. Hastings, it is not; since he has not had sufficient delicacy to preserve silence, it is useless for me to do so."

"Nay, nay; spare poor Hastings; he never opened his lips to me. Well for him he didn't. He confided his passion to Miriam, whose godson he is, and I concluded all was amicably arranged. Have you refused him?"

" Finally ?"

I turned indignantly.

" Why ask such a question ? You know it is impossible I could marry Mr. Hastings."

" I know nothing of the kind. Hastings is possessed of plenty of money, and reckoned a pleasant fellow."

" Do you want me to marry him ?"

He turned his face away.

" Not unless you care for him."

" Then I do not care for him, and never shall. He is no more to me than——"

" I am ?" he demanded, darting round.

My nerve was all spent. I was reduced to a state of muteness, my head throbbed.

" I did not say so," I stammered ; " I— I——"

My remnant of courage departed, and I sobbed aloud.

He murmured something about being

sorry, and not meaning to distress me, and then he got up and walked away.

I cried on, and Rap licked my hand. When my tears were exhausted, I was fully alive to the absurdity of my conduct, and thoroughly ashamed of myself.

I looked about for Mr. Lovering. He was standing some distance off, deep in thought.

Casting my eyes along the hedge, I perceived various bonnets approaching. Church was out. I must make my escape, unless I wished to provide food for scandal.

He turned when I touched him, and showed me an angry, sullen face, passionate eyes, as if all the tears were gathered behind them.

"Oh, it's you," he said, smiling comically.

" Who did you think it was ?"

" The companion of my thoughts—the

devil. Child, how you have cried! Do
you cry like this often, Grace?"

"No, no," I replied with alacrity.

His tone was so full of compassion, his
eyes of genuine trouble, I could not endure
to see his grief. The desire to protect or
comfort this man had taken hold of me.
It seemed what I ought to do—what I
had been sent into the world for. I liked
standing by him silently; such a good
patient feeling came to me, such content-
ment.

But those bonnets : every moment they
got nearer, and I could see a flaming scarf
below a beetroot-coloured face, belonging
to some strapping young farmer.

"Mr. Lovering—say good-bye to me!
They are all coming out of church, and
they will talk if they see us here!"

"Be damned to them! Let them go

home and get a stitch put at each side of
their mouths."

He looked.

" It's the Turton family, arrayed like
parrots, and chattering as fast. If I walk
away they are sure to see me."

" The best plan is for us to sit behind
the stooks, and trust to what you ladies
believe in—Providence."

We placed ourselves and awaited the
issue. Reason as I would, I could not
get over my objection to being seen. I
was not old or coarse enough to be indifferent to the public opinion.

They come on, and Mr. Lovering laughs
lowly at my anxiety. I think he enjoys
my discomfiture. Mischief dances in his
eye. Inspired by suspicion I cannot control, I peep round my sheaf and encounter
the bewildered gaze of Billy Turton. I

hastily withdraw my head and flush to the roots of my hair.

"Eh !—what ?" ejaculates my landlord ; "who has been watching me ?"

"No, no," I whisper ; "don't look ; he —the man is gaping over the hedge."

"He has not seen you."

"I suppose not ; but he has seen Rap, and as we are inseparable, it is as good as seeing me."

He shook with laughter.

There lay Rap, the innocent and affectionate cause of our detection.

"Why do you laugh ? It is no laughing matter to me. By to-morrow it will be in everybody's mouth."

"Let it—I care nothing. And I will protect you, not only now, but——"

He checked himself, and jumped up. Presently he turned ; all colour had left

his face, and he was once more master of
himself. The tone was kind, but all love
had flown. Was he a coward, or a
scoundrel ?

"Let me assist you to rise, Miss Sharland."

The sun blazed full upon me as I stood.
I felt my hand taken and held, and I never
looked up. Without another syllable we
parted, and went our different ways.

CHAPTER VI.

"An autumn day like this hath never been,
   The air is still, no breath doth murmur now ;
Yet rustling far and near are falling seen
   The loveliest fruits from every leafy bough."

THE corn was reaped, the harvest in, and thanksgivings had been offered in the churches. I had gone, and found a corner beneath the east window. I looked at the buxom maidens, the stalwart men, all happy and hearty. I listened to Mr. Duckworth getting emotional over the bliss of matrimony and the dignity of little children. It was all very touching and pleasant for those likely to experience either; but to me, alone in that distant pew, smarting under a sense of rejection, it sounded very like mockery.

The Manor pew was empty. Naomi and Miss Miriam were at the seaside.

I heard with delight the parting benediction, "Now to God the Father," etc., and wrenched my back away from the varnished pew. The people stared at me. Billy Turton grinned; he might have made a grimace for all I cared.

My holidays were over; my trudging life had recommenced; but now my feet rustled amongst the fallen leaves. Autumn had arrived, and the woods were arrayed in coats of many colours.

Danver began to hold up its head. Four concerts were to be held in the town-hall, of a superior grade, and the fashionables were charmed at the prospect of airing their toilettes.

The Woods had a box, and invited me to go with them. I accepted the offer. I began to find that diversion in a moderate degree was necessary. My brain worked too quickly alone in the old house, with only the whistling wind to bear me company.

The concert night was at hand; my dress was new and becoming, of the colour poor people find most economical—black.

We were not to have the box to ourselves. Mrs. Wood had invited the two Miss Butlers, the late rector's daughters; and the curate, the Honourable De Lacy Vane. Mr. Wood was in London.

I was prepared to enjoy myself, and mounted the staircase with pleasurable excitement.

The Miss Butlers cringed and fawned upon me, much to my amazement; the one displaying all her teeth, the other all her bosom.

I was shocked—rendered miserable. The heaving billows of flesh, the gross naked arms and shoulders, from which the shabby scarlet cloak would slip, giving the curate an opportunity for incessantly bending over her, served to make me intolerably self-conscious, and caused some men to turn their fishy eyes to our box repeatedly.

I crouched as far back as ever I could, hiding myself behind Mrs. Wood's ample person; and here the curate discovered me, and began to persecute me with attentions, similar, no doubt, to what he found greedily accepted by the lambs in his flock.

I had never met such a man before. Impertinent and presuming to the last degree; familiar, in a manner offensive. I felt all my dignity rise, while such a sense of repugnance laid hold of me, that it required all my self-control to keep it in subjection. He cross-questioned me with a perseverance remarkable, seeing that he got not one single direct reply. This, however, his dull-wittedness and estimation of his own charms prevented him discovering.

My patience began to subside, my indignation shot lightning into my eyes; and with a retort upon my lips that must have sealed his, I looked up. In the next box, watching us intently, sat Major Grind, the chief of police. His keen eyes were swimming in the water suppressed laughter had produced.

Every word he had heard. My annoyance he appeared to share, but if ever I read expression rightly, his advised me to take no notice of the man.

Smiling in return, I rose and stood nearer the front. Soon I discovered the Leetes in the stalls. Annie looking very pretty indeed. Mary was not there.

Silly though it was, the curate with his presumption and bad breath had spoiled my concert. Vexed and disappointed, I followed Mrs. Wood, and stood against one of the pillars in the hall. Constance chatted to me about the music.

" Miss Sharland, do you know that gentleman has scarcely taken his eyes off you for the last ten minutes?"

" We have not been here ten minutes, Constance ; but where is the gentleman ?"

"There, near the lady in amber satin."

I looked; it was Mr. Lovering.

Quickly all vexation vanished, and I became gladder than glad. I could not help my face brightening, and a smile parting my lips.

My hands slipped into his of their own accord, as if they had every right there; and what did I care for the people? Nothing. I would have bartered the opinion of the whole community for the fast, close clasp of those strong hands— the look of unalloyed pleasure that over-spread his face. Others called the harsh, lined countenance ugly; in my sight it was more than beautiful, because I saw in it every quality I admired, every in-dication of a nature I believed as perfect as any man's can be. His character, by reason of its stern peculiarities and incalculable turns, attracted me. I had met my master.

"I wish I had known you were here," he cried, looking at me approvingly.

"I was in Mrs. Wood's box."

"And I alone in ours! You might have come and instructed me respecting the music. I know nothing of it."

Ere I could reply Mrs. Wood hurried up.

"Miss Sharland, will you come with Constance in a fly? I am going to take my sister and Ethel. Richard shall call you one now."

"Good-bye, Mr. Lovering; I must go."

"So must I."

He came to the door, and stood keeping off the crowd with his arm while we were put into the cab.

We dashed off.

My hand still tingled after his clasp,

when we sustained a fearful shock ; the windows were shattered, and the carriage tilted up at one side. We were impaled on the shafts of a hansom, which had charged directly into us from a side-street. A confusion of tongues and lights, and unwelcome attempts on the part of several street cads to pull Constance and me out of the carriage. The sham jewellery, and breaths reeking of bad tobacco and drink, roused me to a sense of the class of animal we had lucklessly fallen amongst.

They were a new species of blackguard, and I knew not how to manage them. The leering, insolent faces thrust so close to ours, the thick voices offering protection, suggested further impertinence if not checked. Had they been coal-heavers or ploughmen, I would have trusted myself amongst them. But these men were the very lowest and most objectionable of mankind.

I looked for the cabmen. They, having exhausted their curses, had commenced fighting. A dirty, clammy hand, garnished with rings, was laid on my arm. The touch of a reptile would have been as pleasant.

Indignantly I jerked it off, and exerting all my courage I bade them stand aside. Constance was crying hysterically. Another voice followed mine.

" Clear the road there! what do you mean by stopping the traffic ?"

There was the big Manor carriage, with Mr. Lovering leaning out of the window. Our need was too great for me to recollect caution, and I called to him in genuine terror.

In a second he was at the door.

" Now, by all the——"

He wasted no more words, but put us into his carriage.

" Where to, sir ?" asked the footman.

" Home."

" No, no.　To Mrs. Wood's.　We must go there."

The master never uttered a word, but pulled his moustache ; the servant shut the door, and the carriage turned round.　I knew the hard determined expression only too well.

" I have half a mind," he panted, " to take you home.　It is almost too much to expect from mortal.　I see the necessity for a guardian, and I am prohibited——"

I purposelessly misunderstood him.

" The danger is past now.　We had rather a fright, and Miss Wood seems unable to cease weeping."

He turned in her direction, but made no remark.

" Are you afraid ?"

" Not now."

For answer I got a passionate kiss on my arm as we dashed up to Mrs. Wood's pretentious door.

Constance got out hurriedly, only too well pleased to be at home.

I could not, for he held me.

" You are coming home to-morrow ?"

" Yes, to-morrow."

With a bow that was fashionable a hundred years ago, he left us.

CHAPTER VII.

"A thousand steps must a woman take,
  Where a man but a single spring will make."

THE Wood family were in a state of excitement pitiable to behold. Mrs. Wood was
standing in the midst of her guests rapidly
giving perplexing orders, and as rapidly
countermanding them.

The footman had been despatched in one
direction, the coachman, buttons, and
several maids in others, all seeking tidings
of us.

"They're here, mum, they're here!"

cried a number of voices, rushing on before us.

"Miss Sharland," exclaimed the agonised and outraged parent, in the most commanding tone her breathless condition would permit, "how *could* you, at *this* hour of night, remain out, and with *Constance!*"

"I had nothing whatever to do with it, Mrs. Wood. We met with an accident, and were detained."

I felt too annoyed to be explicit, and Constance continued :

"Yes, and I do not know what would have become of us but for Mr. Lovering. A party of intoxicated men pounced upon us out of that public-house in Crib Street, and surrounded the cab."

I saw Mrs. Wood's jaw drop, and her civility returned.

I afterwards learnt that a brother of

hers had been ruined through frequenting that said public-house.

Of quiet appearance, and situated in a respectable street, it was the favourite haunt of the fast young men of Danver, who betted, gambled, drank within its walls.

That little house had its hideous hidden stories of blighted lives and ruined homes, so sad in their silent misery, so reproachful, that by comparison any flaming hell in London stood forth as innocent.

Whether the shabby house had disgorged the demons who capered round our crippled cab I could not be positive, but I thought it possible that in daylight, and in soberer moments, they might each and all be owned by the so-called aristocracy of Danver.

When next Mrs. Wood mentioned Mr.

Lovering to me, it was to relate in a marked manner the strange life he had led, and the reports circulated about him.

She spoke pointedly, as if seeking to impress upon me the true character of my "friend," as she termed him. Had Constance been on the alert behind her pocket-handkerchief?

Very likely; and seen the kiss given that had rushed straight into my heart.

How jealous I was of that atom of white flesh where his lips had rested! how utterly I loved that man in my secret soul! how weighed against one desire of his the world to me was light as air! He was my world.

Without him I could and would live; but I could not live the life that makes all things perfect, and heaven seem but a little way off.

The concerts were ended, and I was at home, my finery laid reverently away in the old press upstairs.

The last concert had not been good, so the judges affirmed, and I concurred with them ; it had not been good to me in any sense.

Mr. Lovering was not there, to my knowledge ; and the late rector's daughters, with the true spirit of Christianity and generosity which seems so abundantly diffused throughout the clergy and their families, had snubbed me.

Since our first meeting they had learnt my position, and were doubtless excessively astonished at Mrs. Wood for having brought me.

Perhaps the unpleasant attention the Hon. De Lacy Vane persisted in offering me had something to do with it. Be that as it may, the next time we met I was as the dust beneath their feet.

The smart these women inflicted only served to remind me of a decision come to previously ; namely, that while I retained my pride I could not visit with the class amongst whom I earned my living. I must associate with those either above or below me.

I reasoned that my pride was absurd, yet I was powerless to alter it.

CHAPTER VIII.

"No, not hate thee ! for this feeling
  Of unrest and long resistance
Is but passionate appealing,
A prophetic whisper stealing
  O'er the chords of our existence."

ONE afternoon I came in cold and weary, to learn that, had I been five minutes earlier, I should have found the Misses Lovering waiting for me. I was later than usual ; I had been shopping.

They could not stay any longer, but Miss Naomi left word she wished very particularly to see me.

I did not receive this intelligence very graciously. I felt little inclined to tramp to the Manor.

Upon second thoughts, however, I resolved to go. If anything unpleasant, it had better be got over; if some good news, I could not afford to keep it standing.

"I am going to the Manor, Peggy," I called, as I pulled the door after me.

Some reply was made, which I did not catch.

Miss Miriam and her sister were busy making up their parish books and arranging the clothing club. They were pottering over it, poor old things, and looking very worried. I earnestly hoped they were not going to solicit my aid. I disliked calculating, and above all, having to tell some other person that I thought their reckoning wrong.

With as much eagerness as a child would display at an unexpected means of escape from a tedious task, Miss Miriam hailed my advent. Her fingers were inked, her hair tumbled.

"My dear, I am so pleased you are come! I hardly expected you would, after such a walk as you have every day. I cannot think how you do it; it is bad enough to be obliged to settle these tiresome books every quarter. If I *knew* that I had to perform a certain task each day, I should never sleep for thinking of it. But sit down, and Jones shall bring you a glass of wine."

"No, thank you," I responded, my heart yearning for, and my throat getting dryer as I recollected, the great cup of tea with which I was wont to refresh myself. "I don't think I will sit, if you will excuse me, Miss Naomi. Peggy said you wished to see me."

"We do. We are desirous of making some little difference in the church music this Christmas, and Mrs. Duckworth suggested what an acquisition you would be. You, with your excellent voice, and knowledge of music, would put into the poor things the spirit they lack, and something special might be learnt. William says we do not march with the times."

I was unprepared for such a proposal, and therefore silent.

"Do you object?" asked Miss Miriam; "sister does not seem to have thought of that."

"No. I hardly think I do; but I am not clear what is expected of me. I have the greatest dislike to meddling with other people's affairs, and hitherto Mrs. Duckworth and her daughters have managed the music, and I am convinced *they* have been satisfied with the issue, whatever anyone else has."

"Yes, you are perfectly correct," said Miss Miriam. "But the proposal comes from Mrs. Duckworth herself. So you see, my dear, you need fear no opposition."

"And why did not Mrs. Duckworth speak to me?"

"I really cannot tell," replied Miss Miriam, looking excessively uneasy.

"Then I can. She knew she would get the refusal she deserved. I will not assist Mrs. Duckworth. Revengeful I may be, I pretend to no excellence in any respect; but I am not hypocrite enough to be on apparently friendly terms with a woman I despise. I will have nothing whatever to do with her or her family, however long I remain here. She has not behaved to me as a Christian—which she professes to be —should have done, or as her position as the minister's wife required her to do. She has only been to see me once—her husband not at all—and that once a visit of scrutiny, so ill-timed and impertinent that I have never forgotten it. Her daughters she left outside, doubtless dreading the evil influence I might exercise over their morals. Her need of help may be great, but it is small compared to her insolence in asking aid from me now, when in my necessity she passed me by with a heartless unjust caution in the form of a tract such as one gives to the abandoned creatures tabooed from society."

"Dear me! How could she!" ejaculated the astonished ladies.

I curbed my wrath, and added :

"At any time I will do what little I can for you, Miss Lovering, but I decline to associate with Mrs. Duckworth in the tiniest matter."

" To be sure. We quite understand and fully appreciate your decision. She ought to be ashamed of herself; and I think she has behaved ill to me in getting me to perform what she evidently did not like doing herself. We have always wished she had a more agreeable manner, and Mr. Lovering laughs at her; but then, he is very severe and uncertain in his humours. He is hardly in the same mind two days together, and it is apt to lead to misunderstandings. That reminds me, he had better be told you are here."

He was told, and came in—I saw directly —in a rattling temper. He likewise had been writing, for a pen was stuck in his curls.

"You are going to stop?" he asked, hurling the invitation at me.

"No. I am just going home; so I will say good-bye, Mr. Lovering."

He looked at me fixedly.

" I am going to the farm myself."

While I made my adieus to the sisters he put on a coat, and we went off. Clear of the house, he turned and asked hastily:

"Who did you meet as you came?"

"No one."

" No one! Are you sure?" questioned he, fixing his keen eyes upon mine, which I had raised in bewilderment.

"Quite sure. Whom should I meet?"

"How should I know?" he responded, with the savage laugh of his I so disliked and distrusted. It sounded like some mocking fiend gloating ·over the strife that raged in the heart of the man tor-

mented. While it impressed me with a
sense of discomfort it roused me to retali-
ation. A spirit of combativeness laid hold
of me, and I retorted sharply :

"You are out of temper."

" No."

We had been tearing along in the twi-
light. I stopped now breathless.

He did not miss me at once ; perhaps
he spoke, and getting no reply looked for
me. I was not supremely glad when he came
back for me. His mood was a peculiar one,
and produced in my mind strange doubts
I could not express. The evil that held him
in bondage had some power over me—
a power which my whole nature revolted
against. I was affected through my love
for him. He might influence me, but not
this possession—this devil, that when in
force warped and distorted his entire

nature, even his face. I looked into it now. There was a quiver round the stern mouth, and some little regret in the eye.

"Have I been walking too quickly for you?"

"You have been going along like an old race-horse."

He laughed genuinely this time.

"Not a bad hit, that, Miss Sharland. I am sure you will agree with me, that it hurts a man to suppress his wrath. Much better let it have its course."

"Perhaps—providing it is the proper one. But I am not conscious of deserving your anger; yet you flew at me with the greatest zest about meeting some person."

"Well, well, I apologise. I thought you might have met Robert Arnot, Esq , of Specklands Farm. Do you know him?"

"Never heard of him. I think I told you before that I knew no one."

"Yes, I think you did" (he evinced delight); "but I thought, perhaps your father might have known him."

The idea of my poor and absurdly proud parent exerting himself to make the acquaintance of a *farmer* so tickled my fancy that I laughed.

"I don't see the joke, Miss Sharland."

"Very probably not, Mr. Lovering, as you were but slightly acquainted with my father. Had you been a friend you might have known that the noble race he belonged to are not likely to find solace or companionship in the fellowship of a *farmer*."

He started as if I had shot him.

"You never told me — who are your people?"

"What occasion was there to tell you?"

"None, I allow; but would you mind telling me now?"

"Not very much. The Earl of Arlington was my grandfather."

Silence for several moments. Then came the deliberate question :

"Why do you not go to them?"

"Because it is their duty to come to me. It is more than probable, though, that they are not aware of my existence. After my father's marriage he had no intercourse with his family."

"Why?"

"His marriage was in their eyes a heinous crime. He dared, Mr. Lovering, to marry the woman he loved, though she was not his equal by birth. My mother was gently born, clever, and industrious. She earned her living by teaching music ; and it was at a fashionable gathering they

met. She was singing to amuse the aristo-
cratic assembly, as I have done, and will do
again. Their story was like many another
couple's, they fell in love—the only difference being that they had the courage to
brave fortune and get married, and were
not ashamed to let their love be seen. I
reverence and admire them for following God's law, for preferring the ' dinner
of herbs ' to the ' stalled ox.' But it had
been reckoned more prudent had they
parted and forgotten their love."

" Tell me why?"

" Worldly people, those sharp and suc-
cessful in it, say love is a mistake, that
money is the thing to marry for."

" You will marry for that, I suppose?"

"Never. But I was talking of my
parents, not of myself. They could have

done with money. It was necessary to my father; he had never been brought up to work."

" This is a queer world, Miss Sharland; and your fate is one of its oddities."

"You do not know my fate any more than I do. It may be sudden death, or starvation."

"Neither," he uttered huskily; "you may have to run a tight race, but you will come in winner. Unless those noble lords and ladies gather round you and bear you off."

" I cannot see what they are likely to have to do with it."

"Nor I; only things have a way of going contrary to one's wishes and expectations, that makes a fellow rage now and again."

The bad humour was routed, and I drew

towards him, attracted as every woman is *once* in her life.

" You are not cross now, sir ?"

" Not a bit. You have soothed me ; this cold little hand of yours, with its firm, gentle touch, would tame a—devil. And I am not that, am I ?"

" A little like one sometimes ; and— and——"

" And what ?"

" You are very contradictory."

" So I have heard before. It is quite impossible always to be in the same mood ; sometimes a good angel, at others a bad one, rules our intentions. Will you try to think as well of me as you can, Miss Sharland ?"

I dare not trust myself to speak. I knew my voice must betray me, and no true woman ever tells a man quite how much she loves him before marriage.

We had reached the gate, and I saw the firelight glowing ruddily on the walls of my sitting-room.

He opened the gate.

"Is it any use asking you to come in, Mr. Lovering?"

"Great use; but I must go round and see Chapman. Some one must go to Barmouth market in the morning."

"Are you coming, then?"

"Not just at present."

"Then I had better say good-bye."

"Good-bye, Miss Sharland, and thank you for your company."

He stood and watched me in.

CHAPTER IX.

"The sea hath its pearls,
    The heaven hath its stars,
But my heart, my heart,
    My heart hath its love."

SOME wise experienced young lady may say these meetings and queer attempts at love were very unsatisfactory. I grant it; but they were in accordance with the man's strange character—rather in unison with my taste also.

I should have been wearied with a devoted lover, who hung on my every word and look, and a rhapsody of affection would have excited my ridicule. I was being wooed in the only manner likely to win me, and the spicy retorts and uncertainty of result served excellently to keep him an object of interest to me.

I was not excessively impulsive, and my confidence in his love for me was now too perfect to render a positive declaration of that same necessary. I was contented to wait. Mrs. Duckworth did not call, and I heard no more of the music !

With the exception of the Leetes, I had no friends. To their house I often went, and they came to me; Mary frequently spending the night with me. Her society was to me a boon. Never being accustomed to companionship of my own age, I had formed a rash opinion that I should not derive either benefit or amusement from it. I now found out my error.

Mary Leete was older than her years, yet not in a pedantic way. Her ideas were natural enough as belonging to a girl of singular determination and intelligence.

One thing struck me as extraordinary, her prophetic tendency. It is called "second-sight," literally it is "first." I have listened to her till all superstition vanished, and I looked upon it as simply the reading of a person with remarkably long sight.

There was nothing sensational about her foretellings respecting people and things. They were plain, unvarnished utterances, that carried with them the stamp of reason and common sense so unmistakably that you were compelled to hearken.

" Mary, how do you know these things?"

I asked one night, after she had told me a person's character and probable career.

" I cannot tell you. Perhaps I understand more readily because I have watched people so closely. I only know that such things are and will be, and when they actually happen I feel as if it was something I had seen or heard before."

I regarded her narrowly. Could her brain be playing any tricks? No; not even excitement dwelt in that quiet nature. The dark eyes had a pleased, happy light in them; the cheek scarcely a tinge in it. Nevertheless I asked the question :

" Are you well? do you think your nerves are not in fault ?"

She laughed.

" You had better not name such a thing at home, unless you want them to think you are mad. My knowledge springs from no unduly excited state of either mind or body. It is merely a process of computation that will work whether I like it or not. They do not suppose at home that I have two ideas to knock against each other."

"But your papa, Mary—he knows?"

"My papa? Well, he may; he has sense. Poor papa! but then he has to think for the whole family—mother and all—so no wonder he postpones the additional burden of me as long as possible. I am not on anyone's mind, I can assure you, unless it is 'Sam's,' because I give him bones, and take him to bathe. Sam is the mill dog, you know, Miss Sharland."

"Indeed, and a great protection, doubtless?"

" Yes ; but I think a strange dog would not be out of place there."

" Why ?"

" Oh, Sam knows everybody too well ; and there is one practice I should like to stop."

" What is that ?"

" That of the boys sneaking out after they have gone to bed."

" How do they get out, Mary ?"

" Through the kitchen-window, and out by the mill. Sam never barks. All the time, you must know, the window and gate are open, and Sam the only guard."

" How did you get to know of it ?"

" I do not sleep very well, and one night I went down to the kitchen fire, and then made the discovery."

" And what did your brothers say ?"

" They do not know I watched them.

I would have told mamma or Annie, but
they snub me so, and take everything
the wrong way. So I just held my
tongue."

" I am inclined to think you have taken
the wisest course, Mary."

She smiled.

" I wish I could be sure of that. However, it *is* no use, Miss Sharland. Mamma
always takes the boys' part, so no good
can be done for them."

I changed the subject. It seemed so
odd to hear this girl expressing wise
opinions, yet scorned by her family, who
ought to have prized and cherished such
an uncommon character.

Mary Leete would be a valuable friend ;
a dreadful enemy. Her affection and will
was as strong now as that of any woman
of thirty. She was attractive—peculiarly

so—having the readiest comprehension and widest sympathy.

Her visits always did me good, and I *missed* her : the first person who had ever made themselves in the least degree necessary to me. I began to wish I had a sister, just such another, intelligent, tranquil, reliable.

Depend upon it, a human being who, having no right to your regard, so appeals to your memory and feelings, is one in a thousand, and above the average.

CHAPTER X

"It may be that no life is found,
　Which only to one engine bound
　Falls off, but cycles always round."

"THE Manor has visitors again."

So said Peggy, and I inclined my head by way of assent.

I might have forgotten the circumstance had not a note arrived; and this was the tenor of it: Would I spend an evening with them, selecting the one most agreeable to myself?

I was not much inclined to make the

desired choice, but prudence whispered that it was wiser to make friends than enemies, and to keep them when got.

Accordingly I went. Mr. Lovering was in London.

The company was well selected, and I found that many of them were staying over Christmas; amongst that number were Mrs. Fantail and Clem.

I was weary enough to be silent ; and, after the necessary greetings were over, I was allowed to enjoy myself in a corner in the manner most pleasant to myself. The one who afforded me the greatest amusement was Mrs. Norton, whose husband—an officer—was the author and promoter of every species of frolic.

Mrs. Norton, a childless young wife, was perfectly indolent. No interest did she take in anything but her dinner and gossip. She devoted her whole energies to these two elevating pastimes: no wonder her success with both was complete. She seemed amiable, and as fond of her good-natured husband as a person of such phlegmatic temperament can be.

She was rich, and that rendered her preservation essential in her husband's eye, who had nothing but his pay. How much he cared for her, I should be sorry to say; as a woman, he tolerated her; as an investment, he prized her highly. My silence and passiveness rendered me a good listener, therefore she affected me immensely.

I did not object, for I soon discovered what a small part I had to play. She merely required my presence, and an occasional "yes," or "indeed." Consequently I was at liberty to drop Mrs. Norton when

I chose, and follow my own thoughts. At the same time I was grateful to the lazy fat creature, for she fenced off intruders effectually. The company were all handsome, well behaved, and contented, owing to stout purses and the means of indulging any whim. Brains they were not inconvenienced with, and yawns would rise which, in my efforts to strangle, forced tears into my eyes.

In a shady corner and screened partially by Mrs. Norton's fat, ivory-hued shoulders, I congratulated myself upon escaping boredom remarkably well. From my fortification I had listened to love-songs in French, German, and Italian, all equally atrociously rendered, and of ridiculous import. I had chuckled at the flirtations that were enacted under the very noses of drowsy duennas, and been rather amazed by various pieces of duplicity one might have supposed beneath the fair maidens.

Mrs. Norton's babble and my watching were simultaneously interrupted by cries of "By all means," "Delightful," "A capital idea, Major Norton."

"What can Charlie have been saying?" gasped his corpulent spouse, opening her tiny eyes inquisitively.

Her chair was a low one, and somewhat difficult to rise from, or I believe she would have gone to see.

Patience is said to be always rewarded, and in this instance it proved so. The knot of talkers descended upon us; Miss Miriam in the centre of them.

"Mrs. Norton, are you good at acting?" cried Miss Rabey.

"I don't think she is," replied her husband, giving her the "go-by" very neatly. "Miss Sharland seems more the style."

Seeing that something was expected of me, I did not strive to anticipate their communication.

"We are trying to get up a play, my dear," explained Miss Miriam, by far the coolest of the party, "and hope you will join us."

"Yes, if I am likely to be of any use. I have had no experience."

"That is of no consequence, I assure you," chimed in Major Norton; "sometimes a great advantage, Miss Sharland. When we are properly organised, we shall spin along famously. The next question is, what shall we play?"

Suggestions were made in plenty, and met with instant condemnation from our leader, the major.

In the end Mrs. Norton proposed a piece entitled " For Ever."

This carried the day, and " For Ever " was decided upon.

There was not very much time, the night fixed for the performance being the 23rd, the Tuesday before Christmas Day.

The dress department was not very difficult to manage.   The piece being a domestic one, our wardrobes would supply all we required with very slight alterations. My character was the least pleasing one, and I set my mind upon having it because I cared nothing about my appearance or success, and the other ladies did.   Moreover, it was rather a melancholy part, and all recoiled from it alike, married and unmarried, probably a little superstitious.

The character is that of a young widow whose husband is drowned while fishing in

Ireland. She loves him dearly, and refuses several offers. It is well she does so, for at the end of a year he returns. He was rescued by some peasants, and carried insensible to their cabin up in the mountains. There he lay ill with brain fever, which so weakened his intellect that he recollects nothing. In time his memory returns, and he hastens home, a prey to the most terrible fears lest his young wife should be dead, or married. Round the poor dejected widow there is a constant fire of mirth and flirtation, very alluring to the young ladies and gentlemen; and therefore the widow was always taken by either an elderly or indifferent lady. It was by no means an attractive character, and when I agreed to take it, everyone seemed relieved.

My reason for selecting it was indiffer-

ence, and the dress. I had no lavishly-
stocked wardrobe, and could not have got
up a toilet suitable for the other characters.

When I had conquered my part I liked
it, and felt that I could make something
more of it. The sincerity, the love that
lasted "for ever," was so exactly what I
approved of that it seemed like a corner
of my own heart revealed, and no imitation of somebody else's. I only came to
rehearsal once, when Major Norton com-
plimented me, and politely goaded the
others on.

My one drawback was the husband
whom I had to embrace and display deep
affection for. He was a good-looking
man — Frank Bancroft, master of the
hounds. I thought he appeared too much
in earnest, but then that ensures good
acting, so what matter?

During my one visit I saw Mr. Lovering. He came into the library and criti-
cised. Mrs. Fantail as the aunt, Lady
Haigh, played elaborately, and drew
from him some well-turned compliments.
My performance he overlooked : rather
snubbed me, in fact, and stopped Major
Norton with a curt :

" To be sure, Miss Sharland does everything well, or not at all."

I was provoked, though I had no reason
to be. I hastened my movements, and
wrapped my cloak about me.

" Not going, surely?" exclaimed Mr.
Bancroft, arresting my hand.

" Yes, going ; in a second shall be gone,
Mr. Bancroft."

" Let me accompany you. It is dark,
Miss Sharland."

I laughed as I thought of the many

dark, lonely journeys I had made. But to have refused his escort would have created a discussion and attracted everyone's attention.

"What, hatless, coatless, in December, Mr. Bancroft?"

"No; I will get them directly."

I let him go, and then I went. In the hall I met the old butler.

"Will you tell Mr. Bancroft when he comes that I have changed my mind, and will go alone?"

"Yes, marm."

This man's face was familiar to me; when a child I had watched him in church. In those days his hair had been arranged with care, and a sausage roll adorned the top of his head. Now there was no hair to curl, his pate was bald, and a scanty fringe of white bore witness to his age, though his rubicund countenance might have puzzled anyone.

Turning from the servant, I saw the master standing listening. He had heard all, and I was glad.

CHAPTER XI.

" My name is Nobody.   What favour now
  Shall I receive to praise you at your hands ?"

THE night of the play arrived.   Intense
cold had set in ; there was every appearance of a severe and lasting frost.   The
fowls were huddled together along with
the geese and turkeys—ignorant, poor
things ! of their pending doom—beneath
the stacks and round the kitchen door
long before darkness came on.   The small
birds sought shelter in the leafless hedges
and trees, twittering plaintively as they

tucked their head and one leg under their ruffled feathers, and went to their slumbers. The Manor carriage was to come for me, and I stood before the roaring logs, waiting its arrival. My dress in the first scene was a grey cashmere, and I looked in my own eyes a very wifely person.

My widow's dress and cap Peggy had put in my box. I was to stay all night at the Manor. Had she dared she would have torn the dress into shreds. Her superstition, her terror, exceeded anything I had ever beheld.

"O Miss Grace! how came you to say you'd play the widow? You little know the evil that springs from mocking at a sorrow; it just tempts Providence to let you feel its weight. God send you may not be the widow of some one in that room this night!"

This speech merited a sharp retort, and I had one on the end of my tongue when a startling knock announced the carriage. I entered it, and was swiftly borne to the house where Peggy's imagination foretold I should repent having acted the widow.

We were not late, yet the avenue was thronged with carriages. There would be a great meeting, and for the first time I trembled at my undertaking. It was but a passing fear; the silliness of quaking at the last moment made me ashamed of myself.

But to remain boxed up waiting my turn at the front door was another ridiculous trick, when my fellow-actors might be waiting for me. I put my head out of the window.

" Can you not go to a side or back

door? I am not certain I may not be needed."

"Yes, marm; if you don't object, we can go round instead of setting down here."

"Then please to go."

We went, and I alighted amongst a crowd of servants of both sexes. There was Mrs. Norton's German maid spluttering and gasping to a select circle of admirers; others were hurrying to and fro with cups and plates.

Somebody's valet was displaying the symmetry of his form in an elegant attitude, with his master's pants and brocaded vest hanging over his arm. All round there was excitement, confusion, eating and drinking, and gossip.

James made a passage for me between this herd of over-fed, impudent creatures,

and I emerged at the foot of the staircase.
There I met another throng consisting of
Mr. Bancroft, several ladies, and Mr.
Lovering.

" Here she is !" gasped Mr. Bancroft,
rushing towards me with so much theatrical rapture that I thought he must be
going to anticipate the performance, and
recoiled.

Mr. Lovering observed it, and a smile
of much meaning twisted his big mouth
for a second.

" They are out inquiring for you, Miss
Sharland," said Mr. Lovering, in his
coldest tones.

" Am I then so late ?"

" Pray don't ask me. I am not affected
with this dramatic fever, and take little
interest in the affair, save when I am required to rouse the joiners to greater

efforts: a thing these gentlemen don't seem able to accomplish."

"Come now, Lovering, give every fellow his due," said Major Norton, who had just come up out of breath and heated; "you know you have a talent exclusively your own for dispersing idlers and infusing fresh energy into their blood."

A burst of laughter followed this observation, everyone being acquainted with Mr. Lovering's method; at the conclusion Miss Clem remarked softly :

"You terrified me to-day when you were raging at that man, Mr. Lovering. If ever you spoke so to me I—I should die."

"Ease your mind, fair lady. If your death alone depended upon that event, you would have a very long life."

A languishing smile was his reward.

She was elated by this reply! then she had read it differently from me. To me it hinted at repulsion too exquisite for words.

With the most bewitching gesture she strove to detain him, but with a curt "Excuse me" he shook off her hand, and hastened away in the direction of faint hammering.

Business now commenced in earnest. The audience was arriving fast. Runners kept startling us with accounts of their magnitude and the brilliant aspect of the mimic theatre. The stage was erected in the second drawing-room, filling the entire archway. Scenery, drapery, and other stage effects were supplied by a man in London, whom Major Norton had recommended.

Had I known the extent of the under-

A WOMAN'S REQUITAL. 143

taking I would never have ventured to take part in it. Innocently enough I supposed it would be nothing more than a well-arranged charade. My ignorance had led me into a fine trap, and I must do my best to sustain my credit. To be overtaken by timidity now would only expose me to ridicule, and elicit no one's sympathy.

A whisper and a meaning smile exchanged between Mrs. Fantail and her niece rouse the trifling atom of determination that had remained latent. I *would* succeed, if only to disappoint them. We were dressed for our parts, and congregated in a room behind the stage, proudly designated the "green-room."

I looked round vainly for the master, in whose stern face I would read some encouragement. He was not there. Major

Norton, under whose guidance we were, had wisely stripped the room of all idlers.

The first scene was in the drawing-room of my husband's aunt, Lady Haigh, with whom I, Dora Hope, had arranged to stay during my husband's absence. Nothing could have been prettier than this scene. There were plenty on the stage, the dresses were elegant, the conversation animated.

My part was not very cheerful. Having bade adieu to my dear Charlie in the face of all people, I might reasonably weep a little behind a deeply lace-edged handkerchief. While doing this, and bending over a vase of exquisitely scented flowers, I surveyed the company. The immense room was full, gentlemen lined the walls, filled the doorways. Even the conservatory was packed wherever a view of the stage was available. Never before had I seen so gay a concourse of people. My eyes ached, my heart beat.

They were all as nothing to me; I only sought one face, and found it, scowling malignantly, with its grim iron mouth compressed, and the sharp eyes fixed upon me with a force that seemed to search my heart for its inmost motive. Was he vexed? I had acted well; I had bidden my husband farewell with as much fervour as if I had loved him. I had looked up into the handsome face with all the earnestness I could muster; and the expression in my theatrical husband's told me it had done its work effectually.

I saw what I had done, and I sickened for a second as I thought how this young man was being deluded to enhance my glory. It was merely acting, nothing

more ; he and everyone must understand
that. No woman could act so with the
man she loved, unless they were married.

Major Norton commended my performance loudly, declared I was a finished
actress, and ought to turn such talent to
account. Mr. Bancroft hovered near, and
whispered that to act so one must
feel.

I was indifferent, too occupied with my
part and determination to crush the en-
vious plotting women sneering round me,
or I might have contradicted him, and
stopped the mischief then. Perhaps I
cared nothing. We all have to take our
spell of suffering, and it was Frank Bancroft's turn. I had endured enough.
That man, capricious as the wind, more
fascinating than angel or devil, had lured
me out of the paths of tranquillity, and

cast me upon troubled waters, a feverish, heart-sore woman.

No benignant power had come to help me; I was somebody else's scapegoat; why not make Frank Bancroft mine? It eased my heart to put my arms round him, and seeing another's face in his, utter the love that was crushing the life in me. I was possessed—mad.

I had always known the danger of bending all the force of my will upon one point; I gained it, and often would have relinquished it two hours after without a regret.

Let me pass over the intervening scenes, in which, small as my part was, I carried every atom of sympathy with me, engaged every eye and ear in that vast company. Anger, jealousy, indignation, fretted the other ladies. They would not have com-

peted with me had they known I was such
a star. It was like acting with a "professional."

I laughed. Their little spiteful daggers
glanced off the coating of mail I had
buckled on, and left me unharmed. I
would gratify my ambition *this* night, I
who had had such a niggard measure of
the world's goods all my life; I would
conquer this time, if never again.

My success did not excite me, for with
it I had pain. I had taken upon myself
the character of Dora Hope, and person-
ating her, I forgot my own identity.

In the last act I had drawn tears from
the ladies by my heartrending grief for
the loss of my husband, the news of his
death having been gently broken to me
by Lady Haigh, who did her part fault-
lessly. In this scene I must appear as

his widow, calmer for the twelve months of widowhood.

When dressed I looked at myself in the glass. My part had so worked upon my feelings that it had wrought a change in my appearance. I was white, cold, the picture of stony anguish.

Major Norton seemed afraid of me. I chuckled inwardly. Had they known my mother they would not have been astonished at my aptness for the stage.

CHAPTER XII.

" Why, her heart must have been tough.
How did it end ?"

My turn came to go on. No nervousness
disturbed me; I swept on, trailing my
heavy robes behind me, my hands hanging
listlessly amongst the folds. My eyes,
large and expressive, told well. Lifting
them, I advanced ; my habitual easy, firm
carriage proved an excellent stage-walk.
No matter how many looked at me, I only
saw one, only acted to one—the man
standing by the statue of " Truth," and

whose massive brow was as white as the marble.

I was powerless to control myself. The wail of my heart, once broken loose, found relief in authorised grief, and I mourned for the love that stood aloof more passionately than any widow ever grieved for her husband. I watched his eye kindle, his lips tremble; the people whispered behind their fans, and the unhappy man who had proposed to me actually shivered in his shoes.

I refused him scornfully; nothing would induce me to marry a second time. My love for my dead husband was so deep, so true, that conscience pricked many of the fair dames sitting there, and put them to the blush. In a tempest of indignation I judged the offer no honour, but an insult; it was but a base woman who could so

soon forget the man she had sworn to love
all her life, and in sorrow I uttered the
words that seemed re-pointed by my
tongue, and turning saw my husband, who
had been an eye and ear witness of the
scene. Straightway my sorrow turned to
gladness, the tears were dashed aside : I
was no widow, but a happy wife, loved
and loving with the love that lasts "For
Ever."

The curtain dropped amid rounds of
applause. Congratulations poured in upon
us. I say us, for Mr. Bancroft had sustained the part of the devoted husband
perfectly.

We ought not to have shared alike, for
our motives were different. He had simply
let his feelings master him, and followed
them. Every kiss, every clasp, was the
genuine lover's. Mine was *only* acting;

and what is more, acting gone through under a sense of insult and injustice.

Hot and vexed, I disengaged myself from his arms, and without flinching dealt him, in the eyesight and earshot of others, a cruel but deserved rebuke.

"My thanks are due to you, Mr. Bancroft, for your generous support, which has enabled me to act in a manner pleasing to the assembly; but the play is now played out, and there can be no repetition."

With a cold bow I passed out.

He understood. What a coward, to take advantage of the piece to inflict caresses and attentions upon me which he knew, as well as I did, circumstances alone prevented me rejecting.

I avoided those I saw, and hastened to my room. I was free, free to let the blinding tears fall.

Stay— I had reckoned too early. A
sudden clap of a door behind me, and
Mr. Lovering was at my side.

"So you would hurry off and leave us—
leave us after turning all the men's heads,
and the women's hearts to gall. A good
many of the men envied Bancroft when
your arms were round his neck; very
likely *he* does not cavil with his lot. You
are vexed, Miss Sharland? I have solved
your pretty, innocent riddle too readily.
Too vexed to speak, even?"

I lifted my face and essayed to speak.
Could I burst my fetters, or must they
kill me? Had he no mercy? Who forbid
a woman to declare her love? why must
the avowal wait the man's pleasure, and
thus offer him opportunity to shake the
faith and courage of the noblest woman?

He looked at me. Even the misery in

my face was not equal to quenching his
anger and sarcasm at once. I could not
speak ; I tried—no words came. I wanted
to be alone, to get away.

"I have been a brute," he muttered,
intercepting my progress ; "I did not know
anything had gone wrong. Tell me ; perhaps I could put it right,"

"No ; let me go."

"You are ill, ready to cry your heart
out. Grace—Grace !"

"Let me pass, sir !"

"That you may weep in secret ; you will
not so much as let me *see* you cry ?"

"No, sir. What warranty have I that
you will not scoff at me ?"

"Your heart. Just answer me this
question, and then off with you. Have
those d——d women been plaguing you ?"

"No matter. I am not inclined to

make confession, so you may as well return
to your guests."

"I begin to see I am wasting my time;
you have steeled your heart. Though, as
I watched you, Grace, I thought it yearned
for sympathy."

I groaned inwardly. This tenderness
was mastering me. God help me, I could
not act to this man!

"Promise you will come back? You
are not going to shut yourself up in your
room. Only come that I may see you.
I ask no more now; the next time it will
be different!"

A face passion-lit, trembling with suppressed emotion, was bowed to mine; his
hands were clasped behind him, else he
might have caught me up as I stood there.

A step sounded. Instantly he became
cold, guarded.

" Do you want me, Pat ?"

" Yes, sir."

He went without as much as a back-ward glance to betray him to Pat.

I had my order ; I must obey. And I loved sufficiently to make any act of obe-dience sweet.

The company were feasting and chatter-ing, but most greeted me with a pleased interest new to me. You see I had amused them, catered for their appetite for excitement satisfactorily, and I had done something they could not do. I had filled eyes with tears that had been dry many a day.

I was not inclined for conversation, and looked about for a portion of the room where only strangers were. An intoler-able thirst was upon me, and I asked the old butler to give me a glass of iced-water.

Major Norton hurried up.

"I have been looking everywhere for you, Miss Sharland.   Lord   Montside wishes to be presented to you."

I pictured a talkative, conceited young man, with the delectable pronoun "I" for ever on his lips.

"Oh, well, never mind him just now."

The major's eyebrows rise.

"I said Lord Montside, Miss Sharland."

"I   am   aware   that   you   did,   Major Norton; and my reply would have been precisely the same had you said the Prince of Wales."

"What is your objection to being introduced?"

"I have none.   I simply prefer to be left here quietly."

"I wish you would consent to oblige me, Miss Sharland.   I feel so proud of

you, and his lordship admires you excessively ; and I wanted, if possible, to help
him out of a difficulty."

" Indeed ! and pray what use did you
intend making of *me* ?"

" Why, you see they are getting up
theatricals at Waterpark, and they are in
a terrible mess for a good leading lady.
Now you know you are a dab hand at it,
and he wants to ask you to take the prin-
cipal part."

" If that is all, you may carry my reply
to his lordship, and spare him the exertion
of coming to me.   I decline."

" Why ?"

My eyes flashed.

" Because it is my pleasure—that is
your answer."

The discomfited major wheeled round,
and I sought another resting-place.

"I heard you ask for a glass of iced-water.   Here it is."

"Thank you.   I am going."

"Where to?"

"Where there are fewer people, Mr. Lovering."

"Then it must be into my office.   Every other room is full.   I know all; I don't wish you to go to Waterpark."

"Supposing Major Norton brings Lord Montside, it will oblige me to refuse him to his face."

"Then do it.   I am glad you declined. I won't let you act again, Grace — you understand?"

"Yes."

And I sat down comforted.   He stayed a little and talked; and when he left me, laughter danced in my eyes, smiles on my lips.   My heart was light; I was happy.

I talked and joked merrily, and soon had a tolerable audience round me.

At the edge of the ring I noticed Frank Bancroft, pale and sullen. This man annoyed me. I was reminded of little H——, who was then travelling in the East.

CHAPTER XIII.

" Gossip, you know little of these times."

CARRIAGE after carriage rolled away through the starlight night, and soon the company dwindled down to those staying the night at the Manor.

I was of that number, and just as I hoped to get off to my room, plump Mrs. Norton dropped into a seat at my side. This dame was mightily pleased. She had eaten a heavy supper, and offered to escort me to obtain some refreshment when she heard I had had none.

"Do you always go supperless to bed, like a naughty child, Miss Sharland? I should never sleep a wink if I did, and keep awake all night. I say, I hope, my dear, you may have softer pillows upon your bed than we have upon ours. You poor thing, all alone; you will have a wretched time of it, else! What I should do without Ned I don't know. I make him my pillow. That is the good of a husband, my dear."

I could think of no suitable reply, so held my tongue. She continued:

"I think it is such a pity there is no young branch to this family. A wife would have a good position as Mrs. Lovering, and perhaps she could get accustomed to that queer man."

"Queer, Mrs. Norton?"

"Yes; and put 'very' before it if you

like. Why, no one knows what to make
of Mr. Lovering; he is never in the same
mind two days running. If you can understand him, you are clever. He is positively rude at times, and his sisters are
silly old frights. But then it is a nice
house to come to, for they know so many
good people, and I hate staying at
home. It makes one so stupid. In the
long run I should not wonder if he *did*
marry."

I stood the blow.

"What makes you suppose so, Mrs.
Norton ?"

"His attentions to her."

"Her ! Who ?"

"My dear Miss Sharland, I shall be
driven to take up other people's notions of
you, that you are fearfully indifferent and
proud. You certainly take no notice of

what goes on round you. Have you not remarked his devotion to Mrs. Fantail?"

"No."

Had she not been so engrossed with her subject, the tone of my voice must have startled her. I felt cold, so cold!

" Ah, then, you are blinder than other people, that is all. He is pretty free when the mood is on him, and rather taking with ladies; but *she* is sharp enough, and unless there was something in it she would not waste her time with him when the preserves are so full of game. Nothing like country houses for making matches. I detest that woman; she is too tricky. If he does not take care she will have him as fast as a fly in a spider's web. They were to have been married in their young days, but they had a little tiff, and during it Mr. Fantail came upon the scene and carried off the sorrowing lady."

I was voiceless. Something beat in my throat, fluttered in my breast.

" I fancy I could eat another puff," remarked Mrs. Norton, shrugging her fair fat shoulders nearly out of her dress. " Come, Miss Sharland !"

" No, pray excuse me ; but do you go."

" I hope I shall find you here when I return. I like you better than anyone here."

Would to God she had hated me, and so kept silent ! I could stand no more : this woman had cut me to the heart. I dared not risk any further operation for the present. My resolve was no sooner taken than acted upon.

I hastened to my room and bolted myself in, determined to wrestle with the

horrible suspense alone. If he was playing me false, I certainly should lose
heavily — I should lose all trust in
humanity for ever and ever. And then
what of my life ?

I sat down, and contrasted our respec-
tive positions and charms, hers and mine.
At the end of ten minutes truth obliged
me to own that she carried off the palm.
They were equals in age, birth, and position, of the same grade in society, had been
friends for many years. Mrs. Fantail was
liked and sought after by the Misses
Lovering. Grace Sharland was pitied, and
noticed by them probably out of kindness.

Was it likely that a man at his time of
life would sacrifice the associations of years
to marry a girl, poor, friendless, little
known and less liked ? No ; it was not.
In the bitterness of my conviction I re-

proached myself for being silly enough to come to the Manor, to allow myself even the pleasure of such an intimacy.

To soothe the smart of such wholesome chastisement came the recollection of indisputable facts, actions, words, which were sufficient to split his soul on the rock of damnation, or transport mine into elysium.

My landlord loved me as well as ever man loved woman, or else he was the devil, minus hoofs and horns. Mrs. Fantail might prance, and display her bosom and teeth for his contemplation : she could neither soften his eye nor inflex into his voice one single hum of the soul's music. Ah, the world, cruel, wise, remorseless, might stand between us, and fate might separate our bodies, but neither hand nor time could erase what was written on our hearts. More writing might be added as years fled by, and eyes and ears got either partially closed or too well accustomed to declarations which brought gratification as brief as false ; but the *first* strange message from heart to heart is *never* rubbed out.

Possessing excellent health and considerable resolution, I slept, which fact may bewilder my young lady readers, should I be fortunate enough to secure any.

The morning broke frosty cold, and the company dribbled down to breakfast disconsolate and peevish. The good cheer provided, presided over by Miss Miriam and Naomi in turbans, brought solace to the vapid creatures, and something like warmth curled round their shrivelled hearts.

By twelve o'clock the stage had disappeared, and music succeeded hammering.

Mr. Lovering was invisible. I wished to go home, but Miss Naomi and her sister made such objections, and begged me so earnestly to remain to dinner, that I consented, rather than prolong an argument which I was unable to sustain against such foes. They did not wish me to think I had been made a convenience of, and that, the acting ended, I was of no further interest to them.

They were delicate in their attentions —good old ladies, they strove to keep alight the flame I had kindled the previous evening, and they succeeded.

Major Norton sought me in the afternoon, and apologised for so hastily naming Lord Montside's request.

" I see my error now, Miss Sharland, and your refusal was just. You are not a professional, and probably regret such a career. But I am enthusiastic in the cause of the drama, and I never saw such a display of talent; and I have dabbled in theatricals for many years. You are a born actress, and could make a fortune easily, and an undying reputation. Some practice is necessary, and private theatricals afford the pleasantest means of it. Do I offend you, Miss Sharland?"

" No. You are recommending to me a quicker and more lucrative mode of gaining a living, and I should be excessively stupid to take offence with you for doing so. Your tone tells me you are aware of my circumstances, and I will not deny that my life is a hard one. Still, it affords me one advantage, a quiet peaceful home. A certain amount of solitude is necessary for the health of some people, science and nature are of one mind upon that subject, and I believe I am one of those people,

Major Norton. A little excitement I can stand, but a strong and persistent hankering after my own fireside to-day warns me that I am deficient in what is termed animal spirits."

"Then you do not repudiate my suggestion on the score of pride and impropriety?"

"Not in the least. Impropriety could only be the result of conduct, and what one sows one may expect to reap; but that is no proof of the ground being bad. As for pride, I do not understand it in your sense. I have learnt by experience that if I don't provide for myself no one else will."

"Your relations, you have some?"

"Plenty, and they rank high; but they will never provide for me, because they will never be asked. I should be ashamed to go while I possess head and hands intact, and solicit alms. My pride will not permit me to turn pauper ; but it counsels me to respect every upright means of gaining my living."

"Will you take the matter into consideration, Miss Sharland ?"

" Yes, I may promise that much ; and I think I ought to thank you for the interest you appear to take in my affairs ?"

" Never mind that ; my wife is quite of my opinion respecting your talent. To tell the truth, you took everyone by storm last night, only one half would not like to confess it, and the other half keep silent from jealousy."

" Come, come, I don't sanction traitorism. Don't create a rebellion in the house, Norton."

Mr. Lovering had just returned.

"If you have heard what I said, you cannot deny it, Lovering."

"I have no desire to try; but being better acquainted with Miss Sharland than you are, I may tell you she is in no danger of becoming an actress, in spite of your pictured victories, and everlasting glory."

"Ah! well, fate sometimes plays the most cautious of us queer tricks, and the fixed intentions of to-day may become the horror of to-morrow. It is never amiss to have a reserve of ammunition when one fights fortune. May yours come speedily, and prove lasting and pleasant, Miss Sharland."

It was a kind wish, but expressed oddly to my mind.

When I glanced into Mr. Lovering's face it was white.

The major left us.

CHAPTER XIV.

" Ah, 'twas too much to be borne ; and he fretted and chafed in his armour."

" HAVE you been far, sir ?"

"Twelve miles or so. Your house is safe ; I saw the firelight on the window. Now, don't get restless. Can you not abide with us a little longer, or has Norton inflamed that imagination of yours ?"

" I don't need to draw upon my creative faculties just now—the reality is too good."

" You are glad to see me ?"

" Yes, gladder than glad."

" Quite right. It makes me better to

bring joy to some one. I am not such a bad man as they paint me; and I was intended for a better, but that merciless hag Fate has been at enmity with me from the hour I came into the world. Curse her !"

"Hush, hush !" I whispered, horrified.

"They have not heard, and if they did they would not care; rather revel in another proof of my hardened villainy. If a great trouble came to me, they would only jeer. And you, Grace, what would you do ?"

"Help you all I could, sir."

"Brave heart, I know it."

Others engrossed his attention, and my place was at the other end of the table, But the ringing voice reached me, and I knew I was not forgotten.

The excitement of the previous evening

had served to stir up the love of it in many breasts, and then came the query, " What shall we do to-night ?"

" Tell ghost stories."

" Ghost stories on Christmas Eve, Mr. Bancroft !" cried High Church Miss Muspratt ; " more likely go to church."

" Would you like to go down to the church and hear the bells ?"

" Duckworth won't be there—we have no service ; but perhaps Miss Muspratt would not object to gracing the pulpit for once, and pointing out our delinquencies."

To my amazement the suggestion was greedily accepted.

Mr. Lovering sarcastically offered to have the carriages out ; this Mrs. Fantail, who generally acted spokeswoman, de- clined. It was a clear frosty night—they would walk.

How I regretted staying !

We were ready, and the order given to march.   Unluckily I had got into the centre of the band.   Some before, some behind, but I was hemmed in in the middle.   Stout Mrs. Norton leant very heavily upon one of my arms, and Frank Bancroft commanded the other side. Poor fellow ! he was nervous and unhappy, like every young man when in love ; and instinct warned me to avoid being alone with him unless I wished for a proposal.

It was nine o'clock when we reached the village.   The ringers were turning out ; and the old sexton, lantern in hand, was unlocking the belfry door.   I went up to him and grasped his hand, the hand that had dug the grave for both my parents.

Poor old man, the tears had run down

his face at sight of me, white and tearless, standing by my father's coffin.

"Have you forgotten me, Andrew?"

"No, missie, I have not; and my old woman was a-asking after you only last night. You're quite a woman now, and it seems but yesterday you was a toddling lassie, holding on by your nurse's gownd."

"Have you been very well?"

"Barring the rheumatis, Miss Grace, it plagues me sore. But I am wonderful, considering as how I have stood about in this damp ground, and dug every grave for nearly sixty year. My grandson, Sammy—you mind him, missie?—is a fine young man, and ready to step into my shoes. It makes me think a bit when I look round and know that where I have laid so many I shall soon be laid myself. Please God, I am ready."

" Tell your wife I will come and see her before this year is out. I intended calling many a time, but very likely you know, Andrew, that my time is not my own now."

" I do, missie ; to speak truth, I never recollect when it was. You were always busy, from the day you could walk.   You'll be glad to know that the vine you helped me to train bore bravely this year, and we made a good bit out of our grapes."

" Indeed, I am pleased to hear it."

By this time the others had come up. The ringers were ready, and a joyous peal rang on the still frosty air.   The bells ceased, and then someone proposed the organ should be tried.

" Who can play ?"

" Miss Sharland."

I was sought and found, seated in a pew

with Mrs. Norton—she talking, I dreaming. I liked this woman's society, because she relied entirely on her own powers of conversation.

Again they were too many for me, and I was obliged to comply with their request. Music never came amiss to me; I lost my own individuality in the sounds, and for a time forgot my sorrows.

The organ loft was by no means a strange place to me, and the organ (old mangle), was amenable to my fingers. I knew how to humour it, how to coax out of its rusty worm-eaten inside some melody instead of gasps and squeals. Many an hour had I spent up there with my father, while his delicate fingers lingered on the yellow keys, and the old church vibrated with soul-stirring sounds. I knew where the music was kept, and how to screw

up the rickety stool. There was only
one candle, but that signified little, as
memory helped me liberally. I played;
they, these creatures of gigantic import-
ance and stunted understandings, listened
longer than could have been expected,
then they fidgeted and dwindled off.

Though I had done a good deal, it was
not enough. Trust a woman for always
having an ungratified desire, a request at
the end of her tongue.

Miss Clem glided to my side.

"Can you play the 'Wedding March,'
Miss Sharland?"

"Yes."

"Oh, then, please do; and we will go
downstairs to listen."

I agreed, and setting the candle on the
floor while I searched the music, paid no
attention to the fact that they all went

and I was left alone. I found the copy tattered and torn. It had never been used since Alice Webb married some young man from London. That was many years since, and about the only grand wedding at Holland within my recollection.

As the well-remembered tune pealed from the organ, my memory reproduced the scene. I saw it all again from my place of observation, the window in the Manor pew; I had no business there—I was an uninvited guest.

I had been enticed by the gay procession which had caught my eye from the parlour window, and without asking permission, I had run across to the church, through the summer rain, with my dolly clasped to my bosom.

When I arrived there the door was

shut. Nothing daunted, I ran round, and grasping the ivy, whose thick fibres hugged the stones lovingly, I clambered up, and thrusting my body through the open casement, viewed the whole ceremony triumphantly. So absorbed were the company in themselves and each other, that I should have escaped observation, but for an unlucky accident.

Entranced by the music and fine apparel, I relaxed my grasp of Mary Jane, who, being but a thing of brown calico and bran, tumbled headlong, with a loud noise, into the Manor pew. Had a cannon exploded beneath their feet, little less terror could have been evinced.

The bridegroom dropped the ring ; the bridesmaids sought with alacrity the protection of their specified groomsmen. The women abandoned themselves to fear with the utter reasonlessness that characterises the sex. They were ready to fly without waiting to ascertain if there was anything behind them.

Now neither nervousness nor bashfulness had been transmitted to me by my good mother, but a keen sense of the ridiculous had, and I burst out laughing, a process that set my eyes dancing and displayed all my even white teeth. Indignation now took the place of fear, and the women, weak spiteful things, launched epithets volubly.

"Abominable child!"—"Just like an imp!"

My friend Andrew now approached and handed me up Mary Jane, and admonished me to go.

I shook my head, took a turn on the window-sill, and remained. I watched the ceremony concluded, and the exit into the vestry. Then I jumped down, and asking Mary Jane how she would like to be married, ran home. I had not been even missed.

CHAPTER XV.

"One string, my friend, is dumb beneath your hand :
    Strike, and it throbs and vibrates at your will,
Falters upon the verge of sound, and still
    Falls back as sea waves shattered on the strand."

THE tune ended with my reflections, and the rumble of the organ as the wind died out of it formed a suitable accompaniment to my thoughts, which had faithfully adhered to facts, and proceeded with my uneventful life. Perhaps I should have gone on through the past till the present had confronted me, had not I become aware that either I, or someone else, had so

disarranged the music that there was no
shutting the lid down.

Slipping off the stool, I set to work.
The curtain was drawn ; the solitary candle was on the floor by me.   Suddenly my
heart leaped, the blood tingled to my
finger ends.   I heard a heavy quick step
on the stones.

"Thought you must all be gone, the
place is so silent and dark."

"So we have, nearly," answered Mrs.
Fantail ; " the young people have paired
off.   I remained, and let my imagination
picture what might have been."

Her voice was tender, slightly trembling.
I rose and peeped through the curtain.
They stood in the light of the lamp at the
bottom of the belfry stairs.   Mr. Lovering
was looking straight before him with
compressed lips.

Mrs. Fantail continued :

" It seems quite a case with Miss Sharland and Frank Bancroft. And she may
count herself fortunate. They strolled
away together fully five minutes since."

" Indeed."

No other remark, but that one word
spoke to my instructed ear volumes.
The hypocrite was determined upon
making the most of her opportunity. Who
could tell what buried recollection she might
not revive, and trick him into betraying
weakness. Men are impulsive, feeble ; a
'cute woman may cheat them into denying
their own conscience. Perhaps she thought
the silence and fixed expression of countenance a sign of inward emotion.

Now she could not read that face. It
was only to her a strong harsh countenance,
often, by the passion that worked within,

made ugly. The big nose, hard mouth, and keen eyes never softened and became beautiful when looking at her. How should she, a creature of cunning thoughts and many schemes, with shallow heart and brain, understand my master ?—who, with the reserve of a fine nature, kept his heart, his ideas, turned from the gaze of prying vulgar eyes.

Mrs. Fantail talked on.

" It is to be hoped she will recognise her good fortune and behave accordingly. She is to be envied—very few marry their first and true love."

He laughed that jarring devilish laugh that seemed like a hoarse scream of strangled rage.

" Be damned to love !—there is no such thing. Every woman is born a flirt, and the more hearts she can wring the happier

she is.   As for marrying their *love*! Ah!
ah! it is not easy to tell who they *do* love.
You did not marry *yours*, I suppose?"

"Ah! William, you *know*——"

Either Mrs. Fantail's emotion stifled
her voice, or mine my hearing, for the
remainder of her reply was lost to me.

A sharp heavy sound recalled me, the
banging of the door.   In my fright I
forgot the candle on the floor, my thick
dress caught it, swept it from its socket,
and put it out.   I was alone in the church,
and in darkness.

Indignation at first routed both fear and
cold.   Presently, however, I began to feel
cramped and chilly, and somewhat anxious
as to various sounds.   I found my cloak,
and put it on.   I parted the curtains and
looked down into the church.

It was all dark, save where the moon-

light slanted through a window, and cast
a ghastly tint on the effigies of some departed saint or sinner.   I could see the rats
—frisky lean, green-eyed—running over
the stones that gaped above the vaults.

The dead lay all under the church, and
time had so eaten into many of the letters
that you had to kneel to read the inscrip-
tions.   I   thought,   were   they,   coffined
under those worn flags, lonelier than I ?

The squeals of the rats startled me, and
a rattling by the organ froze the blood in
my veins.

The moon had drawn back under some
cloud, and my eyes seemed lighted from
below, where the dead rested.   Strange
ideas swept like phantoms through my
brain ; skeleton fingers grasped mine in
good fellowship, as if glad to greet a companion.

I tried to cry out and could not : a dull pain seized my heart, a numbness my limbs, and I slipped down, down.

When I recovered from my faint, the moon was shining brightly upon me, and, secure in her pure light, I staggered up, and blessed God for the lamp He had lighted.

The army of rats were holding an orgie below, but I ventured to look no more.

I groped my way out on to the staircase, and took my stand at the window where I could see my mother's and father's grave. I prayed that the light might not leave that window, that the moon might not be hidden again that night. Surely if nature did not help her child, nought would. I prayed against the sins of the world, the temptations of youth, the danger of setting up idols, and for the man I

loved.   My shoulder ached and smarted—
I had hit it when I fell in the organ-loft.

I seemed to have stood there a long,
long time, my parents' grave and the
moonlight bearing me company.   I must
have dozed, my forehead pillowed on the
window-ledge, my body on the stairs.

A cry awoke me, I started up.

It was my own name, uttered in such an
accent of fear that my heart was wrung.

Mr. Lovering stood below.

" Grace, my darling, I am here ; try and
open the window."

I did try, as well as my frozen trembling
fingers would let me, but it was useless.
The spiders had had their kingdom there
undisputed for many a long year, and
made ladders from the bells to the window
again and again.   The entire frame was
coated with rust.

I tried to speak, but my voice was weak, and I knew he could not hear me. Plainly enough I heard him anathematising, and presently a crashing crackling sound.

He was climbing up by the ivy that twined round the belfry, and some said prevented its falling.

A final swing and he was at the window, only the glass between us.

My joy mastered my reserve, and I stretched out my hands.

Even then I saw the wave of gladness that illuminated his face. To bring that light just once into a man's face ought to make any woman content.

" Go away, Grace! stand off!"

I obeyed. He lifted the stone in his hand and burst open the casement. The rusty iron fastening flew against the opposite wall and dislodged a large piece of plaster.

In another second he was inside, and held me in his arms.

I nestled to him, forgetting all, only recollecting that I loved him.

He chafed my cold hands, smoothed my tangled hair, comforted me by a thousand little actions that a man never dreams of, but to the woman he wants for his wife.

I looked up at him, all tears gone. I was warm and safe enough.

" Is my wife very tired ?"

" Not now."

" Nor cold ?"

" No."

" Nor afraid ?"

" No."

" Then what is she ?"

" Happy."

He squeezed me to him, and laughed.

" Happy buttoned into my coat here,

lying against my heart. Kiss me, Grace !"

I kissed him willingly, loving him with my whole heart. All the ghouls and rats had decamped, and I laughed as I related my past terror and agony. He had found my cloak and wrapped me up in it.

" It is fortunate you had this warm thing on, or you would have been perished. Had I come to find you stiff and stark, I should have wrung Mother Fantail's enamelled neck. Why did you not speak when you heard her utter that lie about you going off with Bancroft ?"

" I was so surprised and vexed, and then your manner and speech—I thought perhaps——"

He laughed.

" Exactly. Like the rest of your sex, you like torturing yourself with jealousy.

What a happy man I should be tied to
that elderly bird!—how devoted I should
be! I can picture it all."

The vision must have been pleasing, for
he laughed again.

" Perhaps she thought I should be over-
come, and in a moment of weakness utter
sentiment, or make a promise 1 could not
fulfil.   An addition to her income would
not be objectionable to Mrs. Fantail, even
though it came through the medium of
the Divorce Court.   Are you in a hurry
to go, Grace ?"

" No."

" That is well, for unless you are agreeable to jump with me out of the window,
there is at present no other means of
egress available to us.   Presently Bancroft
will have awakened that slumbering
sexton, and got the key.   *I* could dis-

pense with his arrival. Could you, Grace ?"

" Yes ; for longer—I am content. But people would talk."

. " They will prate as it is. You should have seen Bancroft's face when I inquired after you. I left Mrs. Fantail to console him, and he evidently devoted scanty time to that most pleasant and easy task, for he was after me in three minutes, and volunteered to get the key."

" I am afraid I have given you a deal of trouble, sir !"

"Verily you have, and some day I intend to remind you of it. Grace ! promise, *swear*, that when I come and claim you for my wife you will be mine ?"

His earnestness startled me, and I did not immediately reply.

" Swear!" he entreated savagely; " here,

where, if there are any angels or devils above ground, they can bear witness against you at the Day of Judgment should you break your oath."

A keen icy wind came in through the broken window : it seemed like a sigh, a chill breath, and the cold penetrated me through. Some icy power held me—something that had neither name nor substance stood between us, and I shivered. Was it death ?—a forecast of trouble ?

" You hesitate, you doubt—quick, speak !"

He touched me, and the cold presence vanished.

" No, you mistake ; I swear I *will* marry you," I answered.

He drew a gasping sigh of relief.

" Thank God ! You have made a noble promise, Grace ; you are brave, my darling, the world would say very brave, to marry wild Will Lovering. Trust me, while I live you shall be safe—with my life I will shield you."

I smiled ; I loved too much to fear anything.

Voices and hammering at the door announced the arrival of the key, and we betook ourselves downstairs.

It was Mr. Bancroft.

He had not waited for the old man, but persuaded him to throw the key through the window, and hurried off with it. In the lane he had encountered some servants from the Manor, with a carriage despatched by Miss Naomi.

" Heaven be praised, you are alive !" ejaculated the Master of the Hounds, fervently, at sight of me. " What a fearful time you must have spent shut up here ?"

"I believe you," replied Mr. Lovering. "When I got through the window she was cold and still, almost voiceless. If it had been either of us, Bancroft, I question whether we should have passed through the trial as well as Miss Sharland. Our sins would have recurred to our minds uncomfortably, and chilled us more than the dampness of the church."

He placed his hand upon my shoulder, and I wondered whether Mr. Bancroft noticed the tenderness in his voice, as I did.

The drive to the Manor was soon accomplished, and I noticed lights in the village as we dashed through.

Mr. Bancroft's knocks at old Andrew's door had not been of a gentle type, and the thrilling account of a lady being locked up in the church had served to lift many a sleepy head off the pillow.

Mr. Lovering laughed, and squeezed my arm, under pretence of wrapping an extra cape round me.

"You will be obliged to drive slowly through Holland to-morrow, Miss Sharland, and show yourself as royalty does. Or shall I issue bulletins specifying your recovery?"

"I think if you would tell your man to drive me to my own home, instead of to yours, it would in any case be better."

"And I think not. You are on the point of breaking down now, and to mure yourself up there, to brood over the horrors of being locked up in that church, would be enough to make you ill."

"I may in any case be ill."

"Then it shall be in my house, where I can see you if I choose. Our carelessness brought this about."

When I wanted to get out I was sick and giddy ; the lights confused me.

The lateness of the hour had scared nearly all the visitors to their rooms.

Mrs. Fantail, however, had not fled the field. She advanced, the dabs of rouge being the only colour anxiety, on some account or other, had left in her bold face.

"Miss Sharland, allow me to express my deep regret for my error——"

The arm that had supported me from the carriage tightened.

"Pooh, my good lady ; if your regret is no more truthful than your statement, which placed this lady in such an unpleasant position, you need not trouble yourself to express it. Miss Sharland fully understands the matter, Mrs. Fantail, and your share in it."

Without giving her any chance of replying, he swept me into a room, and placing me in a big chair, busied himself in divesting me of my wraps.

He forced me to eat and drink, his sisters standing by—then in his own arms he carried me upstairs. I remembered his kisses as we mounted the dark stairs ; he had forbidden anyone to precede with a light, saying he could see ; and then no more, until I found myself in bed with an old woman sitting by me.

CHAPTER XVI.

"'Tis spring that leads them to their goal;
  Thou art the spring-tide of my soul,
  My loved Yvonne, my own Yvonne!
  No truth on earth save love is found,
  All else is but an empty sound."

"Miss Sharland, you must keep quiet; you fainted on your way upstairs. I am the housekeeper, Mrs. Quail. I hope you find yourself tolerably well now, miss?"

"Yes, thank you; and if you will give me a drink you might go to bed, Mrs. Quail."

"My orders were to remain, Miss Sharland, and when the master orders no one disobeys here."

I lay quiet after this, and the old woman settled herself comfortably in her chair.

Presently the volume of "Blair's Sermons" began to jog in her hand, and drop lower; finally it slipped out of her fingers altogether, and on to the rug.

The next sound was Mrs. Quail snoring placidly, displaying the joints of her false teeth.

A piece of very gassy coal was at the front of the grate, spurting out hissing jets of flame, and illuminating for half a second the large room with its heavy hangings, and revealing gigantic and goblin-shaped figures in the corner. I had no weird fancies in my mind—I was amused, not terrified, by the mystic forms.

It was wonderfully pleasant, resting on

that bed of down, warm and safe, after being shut up in the dreary cold church. My thoughts were devoted to my master. I was privileged to think now, and to allow my love to run on unchecked.

I was happy, at peace with all the world. Had I possessed an enemy, I could have forgiven her freely. Who knows the power, the influence for good of a love boundless and strong?

I could not sleep, my joy was too great to subside into slumber. When I looked up, I saw him standing behind Mrs. Quail, his face full of love and anxiety.

I impulsively stretched out my arms to him, and then regretted it. What if the woman awoke? She and others, not understanding the great love that sanctions any action, would judge in the general way, and condemn.

" Grace, you are excited."

" No," I reply ; " I am not. I was quiet until I saw you. You should not be here."

" No ; I suppose not. I should be enduring untold miseries in my own chamber or outside yours, and you awake, looking into the fire, with a face far too earnest to denote a quiet brain."

" But you have no right here."

" I have, and I dare anyone to make it wrong. Oh, Grace, Grace, my darling !"

It seemed half a dream that I should lie with my arms twined round that proud neck, and he, the harsh, rough man, as tender to me as if I were a baby.

I remembered how often I had watched him driving over the farm, and, meeting him, received a curt reply.

His manner had frequently tinctured

mine with acrimony, and we had been mutually disagreeable.

What a couple of hypocrites we were !

The housekeeper turned in her sleep.

" Go, Mr. Lovering—go !"

He smiled provokingly.

" Say, ' William, I love you !' and then perhaps I may."

I said it, and got laughed at and kissed for my pains.

Then he went, and I fell asleep and dreamed of him, as was to be expected.

I was in bed all Christmas - day, for, notwithstanding my protestations that I was perfectly well, I turned out to be a little ill.

In the evening I sat up, and Miss Naomi and Mr. Lovering came to see me. The good ladies had worried me more or

less with running in all day. Poor things!
they had no idea of sickness. Heaven
protect anyone really ill and left to their
guidance!

They chattered and disagreed over me,
until, had it not been for Mrs. Quail, I
should have got nothing. They had not a
quarter finished their discussion respecting
the goods and evils attendant upon eating
chop or chicken, when I had digested my
turkey.

Prim Miss Naomi fairly blushed when
she ushered her brother into the room, and
invited him to a chair in the furthest,
darkest corner.

She had packed me up until not the tips
of my slippers could be seen, and I had a
stout fight for liberty for my hands.

"That chair, Naomi? why particularly
that chair?"

"You would be able to converse with Miss Sharland there, brother."

"Assuredly. I should be able to converse with anyone under the fountain by opening the window and shouting. But I want to see as well as talk. Have you any objection to look at me, Miss Sharland ?"

"None whatever. I should like it."

"There, Naomi ! you see, you need not have taken the trouble to plan for us. We know our own likes and dislikes."

He drew his chair closer, and, taking my hand, kept it, fondling it and inquiring how I felt.

I fancied Miss Naomi looked frightened ; her face wore the same expression as on the night we were in the fernery.

"I feel quite well, and should like to go home. I must be a trouble to you."

He fumed and fidgeted.

"Nothing of the kind. You are a pleasure—a constant source of interest and delight."

He was excited, his eyes glittered, and the head was thrown back defiantly.

He might have said more, and betrayed himself or me. Would God that he had, for then the old, shrivelled woman sitting there had proved an angel unawares. Her cracked voice now interposed.

"Brother, you express yourself strangely, but I hope Miss Sharland will understand. Mr. Lovering wishes to convey to you, my dear, the impression that you are no trouble to us, and in that statement my sister and I concur."

I bowed.

Mr. Lovering exclaimed :

"Naomi, why don't you write for the

'Echo of Fashion'? Your phraseology
is truly exquisite. But if you don't express other people's sentiments any more
truthfully than you have just done mine,
I fear you will not prove a favourite con-
tributor. Miss Sharland perfectly understands what I meant; she is wonderfully
apt at understanding *me*. I think I hear
music below. I am sure they will not be
able to arrange the dances without you,
Naomi. Go. Those red-heeled shoes of
yours, and orange-clocked stockings, will
look to perfection on the floor."

The lady made no sign of moving, and
again the startled expression rose to her
countenance.

I bethought myself of an expedient for
getting quit of them both. To sit there
and know that I was being watched was
more than my nerves could stand, and I

saw suspicion in Miss Naomi's eye. I had repressed my love so long that now it was punishing me by being rebellious.

I must get away—better not see him at all than under supervision. I addressed Miss Naomi.

"I should like to go home in the morning, Miss Naomi; my head aches this evening, and I think quiet will be better for me."

Mr. Lovering looked up sharply.

"You said you were quite well. I shall send for Weston."

I laughed.

"Pray don't. Headache is not considered an illness."

"Mr. Lovering knows nothing of such things, my dear. He never had one in his life—not even the *tooth*ache. We will leave you; Quail shall bathe your head. If you could go to sleep, it would do you good. Come, brother."

Brother went.

When Quail came, my head was better, and I would be alone. The next morning I went home.

Peggy and John had heard of one of the ladies being locked up in the church, but had no idea I was the lady.

"You'll just need to be quiet a bit, Miss Grace," said Peggy, as she settled me on the sofa before the blazing fire. "You might be in a fever, by the look of you. Them churches have given many a body their death."

"Let us hope it will not give me mine."

"Now don't you laugh, Miss Grace. You was always one for hiding your feelings. When a child, if you jammed your finger you'd just wrap it in your pinafore and say nothing. Yours is a stout heart, Miss Grace."

I made no reply. I reflected that my heart, whatever it was now, belonged to another.

CHAPTER XVII.

" We sat and talked until the night,
  Descending, filled the little room ;
  Our faces faded from the sight,
  Our voices only broke the gloom."

To some people how soothing is home !

I slept this afternoon tucked in by Peggy, a calm peaceful slumber. The ticking of the clock, the sighing of the wind amongst the frost-covered trees in the orchard, acting as a lullaby.

When I awoke, my eyes rested on familiar objects, and when tea came I felt worlds better.

It was eight o'clock when Peggy showed Mr. Lovering in.

Having kissed me to his satisfaction, he consented to allow me to resume my seat.

"You were wise to run away, Grace. My patience would have soon been exhausted following Naomi's rule. You will have to invent excuses for my coming here."

"Stay away."

"I dare say. Something is troubling you, Grace; what is it?"

"Are you clever at reading faces?"

"I can read yours. Many a time I knew that my coldness hurt you, and when I saw you marching off I cursed your independence. It was as much as I could do to keep from snatching you up."

"How did I look?"

"Look! brave, cool, high-spirited.

Rarely were you down-hearted. But when you supposed yourself unnoticed, a weary sad expression came into your pale face that made my heart ache to see. And then, when I spoke, how you brightened, and let your fancy have freedom. One moment witty, the next uttering grave tender sentiments that spoke plainly of the gentle heart you owned. I saw that solitude to you was not unpleasant, but that you were disposed for society—that your lonely life was due to circumstances, not inclination."

" I had no idea you were watching me."

" I did not intend that you should have. I wanted to make you love me as I loved you. I am selfish."

" What will your sisters say when they know ?"

His face darkened.

"Never mind what they say, pay no attention to them. We will keep it quiet for a little, Grace; it is better in this case —indeed, in most."

It did not matter to me how long our engagement was kept secret, and I could not see any necessity for finding an excuse for secrecy.

It was our pleasure, and in my opinion that was ample reason. I was averse to publicity, I had no one to please or displease by marrying, no one to congratulate me.

His uneasiness I could not understand. I would name the subject no more, since it was painful to him.

After a few moments I had driven the cloud from his face and made him laugh. Reluctantly he bade me good evening.

"Some day, Grace, it will be different; my fireside will be yours, and then——"

"And then," echoed in my ears long after his footsteps had died away.

It was my first love, and fate willed that I should have my share of dreams and hopes.

He came as often as he could without attracting too much notice, and a diamond ring glittered on my engaged finger.

He met me in the meadows and walked a few yards with me, or waited for me in Danver and drove me home.

I was happier than I had ever been. My friends the Leetes had not been to see me through the winter, for the severity of the weather prevented those unaccustomed to outdoor exercise taking any great quantity. We had eight weeks' hard frost. My duties claimed my attention, in spite of the weather, and, to my astonishment, a festivity.

Mrs. Wood invited me to accompany them to a "Christmas-tree party," some miles in the country. It was given by a nephew of Mrs. Wood's to the children in the neighbourhood.

"You *will* go with us, Miss Sharland ?"

Circumstances had formed a fence round me ; and having no excuse ready, I accepted. Perhaps, on the whole, it was wise to be on good terms with everyone, so I went to Mr. Royden's Christmas-tree.

As Mrs. Wood said, it was remarkably good of him to provide such a treat for the children, a most delicate attention. Why I was included in the party I failed to see.

We drove there in an omnibus, and kept as warm as we could with rugs and foot-warmers. When we did get there, we were evidently not expected.

I thought possibly we had come too
early, for though nearly one o'clock, there
was no sign of the early luncheon included
in the performance.

The house was well warmed, large fires
roaring in every room upstairs and down.

Mr. Royden greeted us in a slightly
constrained manner, and I, being ridicu-
lously sensitive, became uncomfortable, and
heartily wished myself safe and snug by
my own fireside.

Having taken off our cloaks and hats,
we were invited into a parlour, and introduced wholesale to its inmates by Mr.
Royden.

"My aunt, Mrs. Wood, Mrs. Dalsh, Miss
Dalsh, Miss Wood, Miss Sharland, Miss
Temple, Mr. Tudor, Mr. Scotson."

I saw Mrs. Wood and Miss Temple
make gracious bows towards one end of

the room. I naturally looked in that direction. The next instant I devoutly wished I hadn't, for there, squeezed into an old-fashioned black horsehair sofa, sat the Dalsh's — mother and two daughters.

Not a muscle of their sallow faces moved ; they just stared at us, and edged a trifle closer together.

Mrs. Wood spoke, remarked upon the severity of the weather ; and Mrs. Dalsh, craning her yellow, skinny neck out of her ironed black silk, informed us that they had come "Hall the way hout from Heverton in a chaise."

The silence which followed was agonising. Roars of laughter came from the next room, where the gentlemen were; and Constance, seizing upon a handy volume of "The Stage Door," held it before her face, and quietly followed their example behind it.

I turned to the open piano and commenced to play softly.

Talk they would not ; they persisted in sitting and staring at us.

The door opened, and a man entered. Fat, coarse, impudent, with the undisguised impression stamped on his vulgar features of perpetually saying a good thing—the fact being that when not intolerably stupid he was insufferably insolent.

It was Pa Dalsh.

With his mouth twisted to one side, and a leer on his white face, he made a set at me ; and bending till his odious breath heated my cheek, he told me that he had " Nevher met the equals of Mr. Nott's for playing."

As soon as ever I could escape from him, I did ; but I was honoured throughout the entertainment by his addressing me as Mrs. Hays.

I, of course, made no effort to disabuse his mind of the idea. I was only too glad that he did not know my name.

In time came the call to luncheon, which was a capital cold collation, served in a roomy farm kitchen. At this young Dalsh appeared ; an immensely tall youth, with pa's face. We were getting on very well.

I happened to sit next to Mr. Nott, who was an intelligent, educated man, when Dalsh, junior, startled me by jumping up like a Jack-in-the-box, and after nearly braining himself with a bird cage slung to the ceiling, managed to splutter out the wish, while flourishing his glass in true

public-house style, that we might " Hall
'ave a 'appy new year."

I avoided looking at Constance and Miss
Temple, both being terribly distressed by
the evident mirth of Mr. Tudor and Mr.
Scotson.

I was much exercised in my mind to
conjecture where Mr. Royden had picked
up such a set. Eventually, I had greater
reason to wonder, for the afternoon company were almost too much for *my* endur-
ance.

The children trooped in, merry, excited,
and repaired to a room, where Mr. Nott
and another gentleman, dressed as father
Christmas and his wife, were acting to an
appreciative audience.

Meanwhile spectators like ourselves
crowded the rooms below.

The most amusing were, perhaps, the

Wigg family—three daughters, one son, and papa.

They were rich, and all praise due to papa, he had liberally educated his children. These young people were suffocating with their grandeur and learning; and, though periodical resorts to London, and a finish in Germany, had laid on a varnish, it was by no means thick enough to hide the common, raw material underneath.

One of the damsels was engaged to Mr. Royden in a mysterious and melancholy manner. They avoided each other, and he grew furious when asked about the wedding. Their modesty was of a new order—it suggested shame.

Papa Wigg was fat and aged, and never at any time, I imagine, renowned for beauty. His head boasted a few odd tufts of carmine hued wool; his teeth resembled fossils, and ornamented his jaws at intervals. As if conscious of the (thank heaven!) rare possession of such valuable objects, he smiled and talked indefatigably, and laid such stress upon words, and gave them such peculiar intonation, as to raise a doubt in the mind of his listeners as to whether he *was* talking English.

Mrs. Wood attracted him, and seating himself cautiously by her side, he began to explain at great length the present representatives of a once noted firm.

" It his, I assure you, a fact ; there his at present only one hold lady, just one hold lady left, marm. We hold foggies will hall be gone presently, and then the young ones will 'ave their fling. I tell my girls when they want to play Batch (Bach) to me—' Stop; I don't like Batch ; sing me a hold song with a toon in it.' Don't I, Liz ?"

Liz, who owns a flaming red head, and is warming her dirty, coarse hands round a big cup of tea, lifts her dulcet voice in a yell of laughter; and papa proceeds:

"As we was coming along, we met Mr. Handrew with 'is good lady and grown-hup family hall a-going to the reception hin their carriage and pair of 'orses. And Mr. Handrew a-puts 'is 'ed hout of the window and boos."

All praise to Mrs. Wood. She listened attentively, with merely the pleasant smile of an amiable lady on her countenance.

How long we were to endure this inflic-tion I could not ascertain, and my atten-tion was next claimed by a lady (so called) who arrived in a state of temper and magnificence unequalled by any there.

She openly expressed her disgust; had she not thought it was a "dress party," she would not have come, or permitted " Sissie " or " Toddy " to join.

In the excess of her vexation, she pounced upon pretty " Toddy," pinched her, and put her behind the door.

The fun now ran fast and furious ; the afternoon waned, and the approaching darkness seeming to encourage the timid and banish restraint, we unanimously beat a retreat.

It was a cold drive home ; but to gain that haven I would have tramped every foot of the way twice over.

Lonely I never felt, for every evening the scent of a cigar warned me that some-one was taking heed of my well-doing.

CHAPTER XVIII.

"A fool always comes short of his reckoning."

THE weather of course made no difference in my pursuits, and I called regularly at the mill.

One reason for my constant attention was Mrs. Leete's health, and another my fancy for Mary. Things were not going well with these good people.

Mrs. Leetes was rapidly hastening to her grave, and the sons with equal rapidity to their ruin. Their mother's weak habit of screening youthful faults had worked very badly for the young men, and they regarded their father as a natural enemy, from whom their pursuits and connections must be concealed.

Nothing could have been very well worse. Mary was the only one who remained loyal, and recognised in the firm hand a sure guide. The father, finding them so little like himself, was gradually losing heart.

Annie was too weak-minded to take any decided part; and so long as she was not crossed, or deprived of anything, took very little interest in what was going on. Moreover, she was in love, with the probability of marriage not far distant.

Mr. Leete looked careworn and harassed. Mrs. Leete was dying, and dying in terror of " John."

Mary had changed remarkably. There

was a motherly thoughtfulness mixed with displeasure in her manner towards her brothers, that could not well be mistaken. If anyone knew them for what they were, it was this young girl.

It was not long before Mrs. Leete took to her bed. Mary was now the chief stay.

Annie, always excessively pretty and fretful, concluded her share in the house was finished when she had stitched a few buttons on. I saw the light in Mrs. Leete's eyes grow dimmer; I felt the clasp of her hand slacken each day.

The end came as the end of all things will come. She died at the beginning of March.

I called the same day, and Mr. Leete asked me if I would stay a few days with his daughters. I did so; but proved of slight service to Miss Leete, who tormented

the dressmaker and Mary by turns.   Her
grief was so utterly selfish as to savour of
the ridiculous, and that was why no one
sympathised with her, of which she com-
plained loudly.

There was another member of the family
who received a large share of my attention,
and that was Peter Leete.   This young
man's utter imbecility shocked me so that
I tried to hide it.

His mother had always loved him much,
and extolled his "good-nature."   I now
comprehended what that was.   She, poor
silly woman, termed it "goodnature;"
the world, less partial, and therefore more
just, called it foolishness, and the owner
thereof a fool.

END OF VOL. II.

BILLING AND SONS, PRINTERS AND ELECTROTYPERS, GUILDFORD.

www.ingramcontent.com/pod-product-compliance
Lightning Source LLC
Chambersburg PA
CBHW020110030726

47498CB00006B/2043